D1095869

GUIDEPOSTS

The
Angel's
Secret

GUIDEPOSTS

CHURCH CHOIR
MYSTERIES™

The
Angel's
Secret

Nicola Furlong

Guideposts®
CARMEL, NEW YORK 10512

www.guidepostsbooks.com

www.guidepostsbooks.com
Series Editor: Michele Slung
Cover art by Robert Tanenbaum
Cover design by Wendy Bass
Interior design by José R. Fonfrias
Interior cat illustrations by Viqui Maggio
Typeset by Composition Technologies, Inc.
Printed in the United States of America

Dedicated to my own beloved flight of angels:
Anica, Talbryn, Calum, Myfanwy, Kamir
Connor, Bronwyn, Dezi and Adrian.

Acknowledgments

I'D LIKE TO GIVE SPECIAL THANKS to Elizabeth Kramer Gold, the managing editor at Guideposts Book & Inspirational Media Division, and Michele Slung, the series editor of "Church Choir Mysteries." And, as always, to Glynne Turner.

The
Angel's
Secret

LET ME SEE if I have this straight," Gracie Parks said as she cautiously directed Fannie Mae into twin ruts of snow, the result of Indiana's first blizzard of the year. Though her old blue Cadillac's windshield wipers were slapping rapidly back and forth, the thick blotches of snow immediately reappeared. Gracie peered into the failing light and mounting drifts that were enveloping the town of Willow Bend. She was relieved that her adventurous cat, Gooseberry, was safe at home, curled into a ball in his favorite living room chair. "Flo Jackson's husband was the brother of Gladys Martin's uncle." She turned down Third Street.

"Got it in one try," her own uncle, George Morgan, replied. "Lew and Flo moved from Mason City twenty years ago but came back during the summer. Then, without warning, he had a massive heart attack. This is the first course she's taught since Lew's death. I know you're going to like her."

"I'm sure I will." She paused, gauging the size of a small

drift. "I had thought you weren't too keen on making pottery."

Her uncle, whom she and everyone else in town called "Uncle Miltie"—a nickname bestowed because of his penchant for corny jokes—shrugged. "I thought it was too messy and too hard to master. I felt clumsy and not all that artistically inspired. But you know, now I think I'm getting the hang of it. They say it's good exercise for my hands, helps slow the arthritis. Now, remember dear, soften your hold on the steering wheel ever so slightly." His voice thickened with trepidation as his gnarled hands momentarily mimicked his words. "Just let the car find its way, like a horse picking a trail through the mud. Yes, that's right. Good girl."

Thanks to her late husband Elmo's patient tutoring, Gracie was a confident and careful driver with decades of experience and had already instinctively relaxed her grip. She knew her eighty-year old uncle, generally an easygoing passenger, was just trying to be helpful. As her vehicle slowly emerged from the tracks onto a patch of bare road, she glanced across the seat and smiled fondly. Uncle Miltie was sitting bolt upright, blue eyes bright and fixed on the snow-splotched street ahead. His anxiety was palpable.

Since he had come to live with her following the death of his beloved wife Doris, Uncle Miltie's three-step preparation for winter driving was always the same. During the fall, after consulting his well-worn *Farmers' Almanac* for the predicted first day of snow, he would encourage Gracie to take Fannie

Mae into Durant's Garage for a tune-up and tire change. Although Fannie Mae was already equipped with some emergency supplies, step two involved adding extra windshield-washer fluid, a bag of sand, a variety of window scrapers and brushes, a blanket, a flashlight and batteries and a bunch of chocolate bars. "No excuse for not being prepared," he'd say, stuffing another candy bar into the glove compartment. "Mother Nature can be a might erratic."

Then, he would impatiently wait for the final step: the first snowfall of the year when he would ride with Gracie to help remind her how to master winter road conditions. Only then could he relax, confident that he'd done his part and that his adored niece's driving skills were up to par. Uncle Miltie's impatience was finally rewarded on this Friday afternoon in late November. An outpouring of snowflakes had begun to spill from the thick bulge of clouds overhead just as he and Gracie were heading out to the senior center. Within half an hour, the storm had pitched a glittering white veil over the small midwestern town. As she gazed at the garlands of snow draping the trees and bushes, Gracie couldn't imagine Willow Bend looking any prettier. A few houses and shops had already hung their Christmas lights and they now glowed softly, their red, green and yellow shadows reflected in the newly fallen ice crystals.

At last, they arrived at their destination, both satisfied with the short journey's smooth progress. "Whew! We made it!"

she exclaimed, tapping the steering wheel with her gloved fingers. She then reached across to squeeze her uncle's arm. "Thanks to you and the good Lord, I think Fannie Mae and I are ready for another Indiana winter."

He smiled. "You're a peach of a driver, dear," he said. "But peaches are out of season. Can you be a pear of a driver, I wonder?"

"I'll take the compliment, no matter the fruit," she laughed. "That's Pat Allen's van, isn't it?" she asked as she helped him remove his walker from the back seat.

"Yup. She's been helping out now and again. Being church secretary doesn't use up all her energy, I guess."

"Isn't this beautiful!" Gracie said, her eyes shining with delight at their very own winter wonderland. The street lights cast a golden glow on the deserted landscape. The gently falling snow muted the sounds of the odd shout or spinning tire. Every now and then a *thump!* would shatter the air as a branch shed its heavy load.

Uncle Miltie grunted as he attempted to move through the drift. After one turn, the wheels on his walker balked, clogged with wet snow. "Not a lot of moving parts," he said, catching his breath. "But enough to stall."

"Take my arm," Gracie reassured him, fat snowflakes kissing her cheeks. "We'll carry it in."

As they slowly trudged on, Gracie began humming *White Christmas*. By the time their friend Pat Allen had opened the door for them, Gracie and her uncle were belting out the famous song's second verse.

"Aren't we in the Christmas spirit!" Pat said, reaching to brush snow from their shoulders. "I was looking out and saw you."

Uncle Miltie grinned at her. "Thank you, my dear," he replied. "There's no business like snow business—isn't that by the same composer?"

Pat and Gracie raised their eyebrows at each other, then giggled. "Everything's in order at the church," Pat explained. "It's been quiet lately, so before the Christmas rush, I thought I'd see if they needed anyone here. To help out. I'm in charge of games and activities, at least for this month."

Gracie looked around the room. For such a bad-air day, as Uncle Miltie might say, the weather wasn't keeping people away.

Pat waved at another volunteer. "Everyone seems to have plenty to do, even if they can't go outside to make snowmen or even shovel the walk. You can't break your hip playing checkers!"

"You're right," Gracie agreed. "But when the snow stops, someone needs to clear the path from the door!"

"Actually, as I was watching you two caroling your way from Fannie Mae, I was realizing I'd better go lay down a bag or two of salt."

"The folks in this place will never know what hit them,"

Uncle Miltie whispered as the ever-efficient secretary scurried away. "Now, come on. I want you to meet Flo."

They found Florence Jackson in a small back room cluttered with low tables lining the walls and overflowing with molds, pieces of ceramic and small jars of paint. A large firing kiln hugged the back wall. Four pottery wheels filled the center, one spinning and spitting water. Gracie's eyes were immediately drawn to the long-haired woman hunched over the rotating wheel. She glanced up with a brief smile as they entered, then immediately returned to her work. Her foot worked the pedal, strands of her hair dancing while the wheel hummed.

Gracie watched, fascinated, as a swirling lump of wet red clay bobbled and wobbled crazily, slowly changing into a gyrating ball. Then as Flo slid her slender fingers up and down and pushed her thumbs into the mass, it spun, grew taller, then squatter. Suddenly, the clay magically transformed into an elegant vase. The spinning slowed. Gracie shook her head in awe as a slender, curving neck emerged and then, after a quick push-pull movement, an upturned lip and graceful spout appeared. Just as Gracie put her hands together to applaud, Flo frowned. The wheel wheezed, then slowed. The potter's strong fingers stabbed down sharply. Gracie glanced at her uncle whose face remained passive, as though he had seen this dramatic turn of events before. The vase suddenly collapsed into a spiraling uneven blob. Unconsciously, Gracie sighed.

The wheel stopped whirling. Florence cleaned her hands in a nearby sink, then began wiping them on a dirty paint-stained smock as she rose from her stool. Gracie's eyes were glued to the vase, still startled by what she'd just seen.

"Gracie Parks, I'd like you to meet Florence Jackson," Uncle Miltie said.

Finishing drying her hands on another towel, the potter extended a slender palm. "Call me Flo, please." Her voice was soft and pitched low. "It's hard to believe we've not run into one another before now. Willow Bend's proud of you, I know, but it's nothing compared to how your uncle feels."

"It's my pleasure," Gracie replied. "My uncle can't stop talking about you, either. Please forgive me for asking but what happened?" She pointed to the lump. "I've never seen anyone create anything so beautiful before and then . . ." She hesitated, uncertain what to say.

"Oh, that," Flo replied, throwing a damp cloth over the wheel. "It just wasn't right. No use continuing then, is there, Uncle Miltie?"

He shook his head.

"That's the wonderful thing about working with clay rather than something harder, less forgiving, like glass or wood." She picked up a blob of red mud from the floor and rubbed it tenderly through her fingers. Gracie watched as her hazel eyes seemed to light from within. "It's elastic, extremely pliable, yet it'll retain a shape. A potter's clay has its own energetic balance. Isn't that right, Uncle Miltie?" The old man nodded, transfixed by her words. Florence's fingers moved quickly. "It's alive, just like you and me." She handed the bit of clay to Gracie, who stared in wonder. Florence Jackson had fashioned a miniature of the vase she had just destroyed.

"Your uncle's doing very well," Flo said. "He's one of my most enthusiastic students."

Uncle Miltie blushed slightly, then began clearing a space on a nearby table.

"I'm hoping he'll show me some of his work," Gracie said. "So far, he's been very mysterious."

Flo glanced at the elderly man and smiled. "Oh, you have to allow us our creative vanity. I encourage all my students not to discuss or show their work prematurely. Extremely dangerous, you know. Artists must fiercely protect their energies and secrets until the time is right. That connection to the creative process is very tenuous, very fragile." She pulled an errant hair into place. "Not something to treat lightly."

Gracie didn't really fully understand what Florence was saying, but she nodded encouragingly. She was always pleased to see her uncle interested and active.

"Would you like to come look?" Uncle Miltie asked.

"I thought you'd never ask," Gracie replied, taking his arm.

Within minutes, Gracie felt even more at a loss as her uncle proudly showed her the workings of a pottery wheel, the different pails of ready-made clay, the astonishing rainbow of glazes and washes, the variety of brushes and sculpting tools and a bookshelf bursting with molds of every shape and size. When they finally reached the firing kiln, her mind was reeling, much like the spinning lump of clay Flo had uncovered and begun to reshape. Then, just as Uncle Miltie pulled open the door to the kiln, a scream from outside the room snapped the hairs on Gracie's neck to attention.

"My bracelet!" a woman's voice shrieked. "My bracelet! Someone's stolen my emerald bracelet!"

GRACIE WAS THE FIRST to reach the woman who was shouting. She recognized her as Libby Simmons, Marybeth Bower's mother. Tears were streaming down her wrinkled cheeks. Though small and frail, her voice was surprisingly strong, and she kept shrieking "Thief!" while peering at her wrist and shaking her head. A group of men and women were looking on, their faces blank with shock. Others soon appeared, drawn by the commotion.

"It's gone," she sobbed. "Stolen. Call my son-in-law. He'll know what to do."

Startled whispers bounced around the room.

"There, there," soothed Gracie. She wasn't sure the best thing to do was to phone Herb Bower without taking a little time to assess the situation. Though his wife, Marybeth, was both a friend and a member of Gracie's church choir, Herb was still the chief of police and undoubtedly had other things to occupy him in the midst of a blizzard. "I'm sure we don't have to bother the police."

As Gracie knelt beside Libby and rummaged for a tissue from her purse, a small crowd closed in. Gracie heard the clumping sound of her uncle's walker approaching.

"What's going on?" an authoritative voice commanded. The knot of onlookers relaxed and Molly Cook, the center's coordinator, marched through. "Libby, what's wrong? You all right?"

The elderly lady looked up at her with a stricken expression. "It's my bracelet, Molly. Someone's stolen it." She thrust out a thin wrist. "See, it's gone."

"Again? Are you sure?"

"What do you mean *again*?" Gracie asked, softly patting Libby Simmons's hand.

Molly glanced at her. "Gracie! Oh, hello. I didn't realize it was you. Well . . ." She seemed to notice the crowd for the first time. Pat Allen caught her look and began herding people away. Molly turned back. "Well, um, you see," she started awkwardly. "It's happened before. Several times, hasn't it, Libby?"

The elderly woman said only, "Call Herbie. He'll find it." She clamped her lips tightly, as if to hold in her distress.

"You mean it's been stolen before?" Gracie asked, her voice rising as she stood up. Her uncle moved to her side.

"Stolen? Good heavens, no!" Molly replied, glancing

quickly around. "Nothing like that! We don't need the police. Not yet. The bracelet's, uh, got a tricky clasp, doesn't it, Libby? Catches on things and falls off. It's happened before. We'll probably find it on the floor or caught on a piece of furniture." She knelt beside Mrs. Simmons. "How about we take a good look round, all right? I'm sure we'll be able to find it. We've never had anything stolen around here. Nothing like that."

She clapped her hands firmly, clearing her throat. "Excuse me!" she shouted. "May I have your attention!" Pat Allen's face peered from the games room, then disappeared. A moment later, she reappeared, accompanied by half a dozen seniors. Gracie watched, hiding her amusement, as Pat efficiently began rounding up people. Soon the visitors, volunteers and staff were all assembled in the room, whispering among themselves.

"Thank you," Molly told them, her voice clear and loud. They fell silent. "Mrs. Simmons has lost—er—at least, her bracelet is missing."

"Oh, not again." Gracie recognized the speaker as a cousin of Lester Twomley, one of her fellow choir members.

"Now, now," Molly continued. "It's very valuable to Mrs. Simmons. It's a gold band with a single emerald in the middle."

"Oh, we *all* know what it looks like." Gracie knew this speaker, too—it was Ann O'Neil's father.

Molly frowned. "I think if we work together, we can find it. Right? Okay." With good-humored dispatch, she and Pat organized everyone into groups, and then divided the building into small areas. Each group was assigned its own tiny area to scrutinize.

Gracie, along with her uncle and Flo, began a deliberate sweep of the area around the front entrance. Uncle Miltie made his way slowly while the two women surveyed the floor and rubber matting where boots were lined up like soldiers on parade.

"Why did Mozart sell his chickens?" Uncle Miltie whispered.

"Oh no, Uncle Miltie," Gracie responded, her voice a soft warning.

Flo gave him a surprised glance. "No idea."

Eyes on the carpet, Uncle Miltie replied, "Because they ran around cackling, 'Bach. Bach. Bach.'" He paused, waiting for their reaction.

Flo and Gracie suddenly felt like old friends.

"That joke was so old when I first heard it," Uncle Miltie continued, "the Dead Sea was only—"

"Sick!" The two women replied simultaneously.

The trio burst out laughing, then paused as several heads twisted in their direction.

"Found something?" Molly's voice rang out.

"No," Gracie called. "Sorry!" She bumped into something.

"Oh!" a voice cried.

Startled, Gracie glanced up into a young woman's face. "Pardon me," she said, realizing that she had walked into the girl's path. "I didn't see you."

"I didn't steal it!" the teenager said in a rush, her voice rising at the end of the sentence. She wore a blue smock over her jeans and sweater and carried a broom. Her brown eyes opened wide. "Honest! I've never stolen anything in my life."

Gracie paused. "But no one's said you did, dear," she finally replied. "No one says it's even stolen . . . it's probably just been mis—"

"Bridget!" Molly Cook's voice broke in. She paused beside Gracie.

The girl jumped. "Yes, Mrs. Cook?"

"It's a mess here today. Best if you keep on with your work. We don't want another little problem, now, do we?" Bridget's pretty face reddened. "And keep your eyes open for Mrs. Simmons's bracelet. You know she's lost it?"

The girl's jaw tightened. "Yes, Mrs. Cook," she replied, then moved away quickly.

"Anyone found anything?" Molly asked.

"Two pennies and a button," Uncle Miltie replied, handing them over. "Not much of a haul."

"Anyone else?" Flo asked.

Molly shook her head. "You finished along here? If so, thanks for your help. I'll go check with the others now."

Gracie, her uncle and Flo Jackson returned to the room a

few minutes later to listen to Molly as she made a progress report. "No luck so far," she informed them all. "But we'll keep looking—right, everyone?"

A few voices mumbled an acknowledgment. "Don't worry, dear. It'll turn up," a stout woman said, patting Libby Simmons on the shoulder. "It always does."

"Is the bracelet very valuable?" Flo asked Molly.

The tall woman shook her head. "Mostly sentimental, but the emerald's real. It was given to her by her late husband, I understand."

Gracie turned to Molly. "Are you going to call Herb? He *is* her son-in-law."

Molly Cook paused, then exhaled. "I don't think so. Not just yet. We did the first time, you see. Straight away." She frowned at the memory. "He came right over and it didn't take him five minutes to find it. The poor dear had dropped it while leaving the library. Since then, she's lost it twice. Both times we found it within a day. I think I'll wait, just to be sure. I don't like to bother him unnecessarily."

"Makes sense to me," Uncle Miltie said. "Well, if you'll excuse me, ladies," he added, turning his walker. "I'm feeling a creative urge coming on. Don't worry about me getting home, Gracie. I'll find my own way." With a mock salute, he headed toward the pottery room.

"Think I'll do a little more checking," said Molly, heading off down the hall.

Gracie smiled at Florence. "Well, this didn't give us much

time to chat. You'll have to come for tea sometime. Will you?"

The other woman started, as though pulled back from thoughts far away.

"Tea? Why, it's just what I need! Where shall we go?"

Gracie paused and was about to explain to Florence that she had misunderstood when she noticed the younger woman's eyes. They were glistening with tears. Then she saw her fingers moving, stroking her wedding band. Gracie could have kicked herself. She'd forgotten that Flo was newly widowed. She remembered all too well the raw pain that had haunted her the year following Elmo's unexpected death and that could hit so unexpectedly.

Gracie smiled. "It's pretty awful outside. I think we'll have to settle for the vending machines and some cardboard-flavored water."

It was the potter's turn to smile. "I'm not fussy. Half the time, my cup's laced with clay. Anything hot is fine by me."

"It's so small," Flo said, carrying her cup and a packet of cellophane-wrapped cookies to a small table. "Sometimes I can't breathe, I feel so constricted." She set down what she was holding and pulled a chair out for Gracie. Gracie stopped to grab some napkins and sugar packets before joining her new friend.

"It must be very hard," Gracie said sympathetically. "Living in an apartment when you're used to more space."

"It's terrible! Not only is there not enough room for my work, my pottery wheels and my kilns, I need space . . . me," Flo said, her fingers placed over her heart. "To be able to move. I just *can't* be creative otherwise. But after Lew's . . ." Her shoulders sagged. "Well, on my own, the house was too . . . I know, on some level, I understood how much he did, you know, fix-it jobs, but it wasn't until . . ." She paused, catching her breath.

Gracie nodded slightly. "I was fortunate. After my Elmo's passing, I was afraid I might have to give up my home. There's so much to do and it seems so *big* . . . empty when you're by yourself. I was trying to prepare myself to leave . . . but then, after a while," she hesitated, smiling at the thought. "Uncle Miltie moved in. We make a pretty good team, really. He's very handy, fixes all sorts of things around the house. Just the way Elmo always *meant* to." She smiled. "He's good company, too. We care about each other."

Flo nodded, taking a bite of a cookie and offering one to Gracie. "He thinks the world of you, you know. Talks about you all the time." She sighed, staring into her tea. "You're very lucky."

"I know," Gracie replied simply, pouring milk. "The dear Lord watches over me." She touched Flo's hand. "He watches over you, too, you know."

Her companion's eyes narrowed. "He does more than watch," she replied bitterly. "First, He *stole* my husband from me, then my home. And with it, my only way of dealing with … with …" Her voice caught. "Without my art, I … can't forget or move on. Never mind that without my own kiln, I've lost the only way I know how to earn money. Now, I teach a class or two—which doesn't really even pay for my time— just so I can occasionally use the center's kiln." Flo shook her head sadly. "I'd just as soon God left me alone, Gracie, and watched someone else. Do you understand? He's been no help to me. None whatsoever."

Gracie tried to hide her shock. "Oh, Flo, I'm so sorry you think that way. I know it's hard to accept the loss of a loved one. My Elmo's death made no sense to me, that's for sure." She drew a deep breath, then glanced upward. "But I know He's got a plan, mysterious as it may be to us. He understands the reasons. Remember: *Be not afraid, neither be thou dismayed: for thy Lord thy God is with thee, whithersoever thou goest.*"

"I'm not sure I want Him with me anymore."

Gracie caught her breath sharply, causing Flo to pause. "I'm sorry, Gracie, but I just can't see the future as being anything but dismal. And it's all His fault." Florence Jackson stood suddenly. "Thank you for the company. I've got some cleaning up to do." Her heart heavy, Gracie watched the potter head off without looking back.

Walking to the hallway, she took her coat and soft wool muffler, debating whether she needed the earmuffs she had in her pocket. Waving goodbye to a pair of men, Gracie then stepped into the brisk air.

The snowfall had stopped. The parking lot was carpeted in shimmering ice crystals. After brushing off a blanket of snow, she opened the driver's door and started Fannie Mae's engine. As it warmed up, she got out to brush off the rest of the car. As she did so, she silently prayed.

I know You have the weight of the entire world in Your hands, dear God, so I'll keep this short. I really just want to thank You. I admit, when Elmo died, I felt abandoned, just like Flo. But it didn't take long, dear Lord, for me to hear Your voice again.

She traced a heart in the snow covering her windshield, then wiped it off with an embarrassed chuckle. The cold numbed her cheeks. *I heard You clearly in Pastor Paul's sermons, in Uncle Miltie's laugh, even in my sweet Gooseberry's purring. It was You who arranged for Uncle Miltie to live with me. For that, I will be eternally grateful. Yes, dear Lord, You take away, but You also give. You have blessed me with a wonderful family, friends and the ability to keep my own home.*

She popped the long-handled brush into the back seat and climbed into the car's warmth. *I hope You can do something for Florence. Now she only sees the darkness,* Gracie thought as she flicked on the headlights. *Help me to help her see Your light.*

The inkling of an idea crept into her head.

I'M SO GLAD YOU LIKED FLO," Uncle Miltie told her later that evening as he began to set the table. "She could use a friend. I think she's very lonely. Foolish woman, really. Because she pretends *not* to be, spouting all sorts of nonsense about needing space to be creative. But I see it in her eyes— she watches. And when she sees a couple talking or laughing, especially laughing, they go very dark. Not everyone understands her, you know."

"She's going through a rough time, poor dear. Lots of adjustments," Gracie replied, opening a jar. She tried not to look surprised at how personally involved her uncle seemed to be with Florence Jackson. "Grieving's very difficult. Everyone has their own way."

Uncle Miltie stared at his niece for a long moment. "Yes," he said tenderly. "Guess we both know what's she's going through."

Gooseberry, her pumpkin-colored companion, now appeared. First twining himself through Gracie's legs, he then sauntered over to his water dish. He began drinking, gracefully dipping his large head.

"*Hmm*, those spicy pork chops sure smell divine," Uncle Miltie said, sniffing. "I see we're having that delicious yellow rice flavored with—what'd you call it—sage?"

Gracie was slicing green olives. "Close. It's saffron. One's an herb and one's a spice."

"Saffron, sage, parsley, thyme . . . they're all the same to me, dear. It's what you do with them that I understand."

He departed for the dining room. Gooseberry meowed loudly. Gracie glanced over at him and chuckled. The fluffy cat was sitting smack dab in front of his empty food dish, whiskers twitching in anticipation. "Just a minute, sweetie," she said, glancing at her kitchen clock: 4:36 P.M. Her guests were arriving in an hour.

She ran a mental check list. The meat would be ready at six, the baguette of fresh French bread and slab of garlic butter were already in the dining room, along with candles and a vase of dried flowers. The table was being set. The mile-high lemon meringue pie she'd made in the morning waited on the counter. The rice and vegetables would soon be in the oven in a tightly closed baking dish.

Given the road conditions, it was very likely her male guests would be late. Marge would be right on time, as usual.

It took more than a couple of snowdrifts to thwart her next-door neighbor. She smiled at the image of her best friend stalwartly crossing their adjoining snow-piled lawns. She poured some dry food into Gooseberry's bowl, then stroked him for a moment as he began to eat. Yes, she thought, everything's in order. With a satisfied sigh, she reached into the vegetable bin of the refrigerator, pulled out broccoli and carrots and began chopping.

"Will you be getting some fresh flowers?" her uncle asked, suddenly reappearing.

Gracie shook her head.

Uncle Miltie's blue eyes blinked rapidly. "But you always have them when guests are coming."

"Not tonight. The roads were slippery, so I didn't bother going by the Willow Mart." She glanced up. "Don't you like the dried flower arrangement?"

"It's fine. It's just... well, you're not going out?"

Gracie shook her head, carrot peelings flying as she rhythmically scraped. "Everything's all set."

Her uncle frowned. "You've got my standards set too high. It won't be the same without fresh flowers." He looked at his watch. "You've got time, you know. I can finish fixing the vegetables for you."

"Thanks for the offer but, really, the table will be fine, just the way it is."

Uncle Miltie paused. "If that's the way you want it," he replied finally. It was clear that he didn't agree.

Gracie was about to ask him why he was suddenly so concerned about the niceties of table decorations when her kitchen timer went off. She reached for her oven mitts. "Why don't you watch some TV? Might be an update on the storm."

"You having a shower before dinner?"

She ran a hand across her red curls. "No," she answered, smiling at him. "You go ahead if you want. I'll just need to freshen up a bit."

Uncle Miltie shook his head, then hesitated, as if he were about to say something. After a minute, he sighed heavily, then slowly turned and tramped into the living room. In a moment, Gracie heard the usual cacophony of voices coming from the television.

It took her another fifteen minutes to finish chopping the vegetables and garlic cloves, measure out the rice and pour the chicken broth. Just as she was closing the oven door, she heard a muffled thump. She paused. "Uncle Miltie?" she called. There was no reply other than the blaring sound of the TV.

The unknown noise had come from outside. Running her hands across her apron, she moved to the window and peered into the barren snowscape. Her lawn and gardens looked as though they had been covered in white cake frosting. A dusting of snowflakes sparkled across her drive and along the narrow sidewalk strip where she had shoveled earlier. Normally, she wouldn't have bothered tackling the driveway, knowing that it would be cleared by Harry Durant early the next morning. It was part of a deal she had struck with the local owner of the Gas-and-Go in exchange for some home-cooked meals. But today she had pushed herself to clear a parking spot for her guests. The street seemed deserted and dim, save for the soft twinkling of the Hadlocks' Christmas lights. As she was turning away, she heard another bang.

Very close by.

Her breath coming faster, Gracie tugged on an old overcoat, shoved her feet into a pair of wool-lined rubber boots at the back door, then boldly tramped outside.

In the brightness cast by the back-door floodlight, she noticed an inky set of footprints staining the pearly landscape. The tracks headed directly to her garage. As she stepped into them, a scuffling sound caught her attention.

She whirled. A shadowy figure was sprinting across the street. "Hey!" she shouted, heart lurching into throat.

The figure froze, then turned. A boy's face stared at her. Then, he bent down and began furiously shoveling Hallie Finkmeyer's driveway.

"Hello!" she shouted.

The boy waved but kept to his task.

Gracie caught her breath and headed to her garage. The door was open, a beam of light spilling onto the snow. Just as she peered inside, she was once again startled by a streaking movement. "Oh!" she shrieked. Gooseberry scooted by, pumpkin pie à la mode recast in fur and ice crystals.

Hunched over his small workbench in the corner, Uncle Miltie jerked upright. "Who's there?" he demanded, pushing something into the shadows.

Gracie gulped, then found sufficient breath to laugh. "Just me," she replied, entering the garage. Her uncle stood in the shadow cast by the bare bulb overhead. He shifted nervously, hands behind his back. "I heard a noise and came out to investigate. I was surprised by some boy dashing across the road. You all right?"

Uncle Miltie nodded. "Just thought I'd check the Christmas lights," he replied after a moment.

"What happened? You drop something?"

The elderly man hesitated, then slipped deeper into the shadows. "It's that darned cat of yours. Came flying in here, rushing around like a boomerang. Must have knocked something over." His arm moved. Gracie heard a tinkling sound, then saw Uncle Miltie hold up a soft drink can. "Here's the culprit."

"Well, as long as you're all right," Gracie said. She reminded him of the time before heading back to her kitchen.

She wasn't sure why he was acting strangely, but, as she tramped through the snow, an odd thought struck her. Probably just wanted a bit of space himself. Perhaps she had been crowding him all along. Maybe that's why her uncle had been mentioning Flo so often. Gracie vowed to give him more breathing room in the future. After all, she realized, Florence Jackson might not be the only one who craved an extra measure of privacy.

"You know, Gracie, " Pastor Paul Meyer said, taking a moment to cut a bite of pork chop. "It's a good thing my mother's still in Honduras doing missionary work or she'd be mighty upset by what I'm about to confess."

Gracie, her uncle and the other guests waited expectantly.

"Don't you dare tell her, but these are the best pork chops I've ever tasted."

"Wait a minute! Your mom was always telling us her cooking left a good deal to be desired!" Marge Lawrence reminded him. Gracie grinned across the dining room table at her friend. Tonight, Marge's hair was swept back into a softly pillowed bun. A few strands tumbled across her forehead, enhancing the overall affect. Her lips and nails were a matching deep pink, dramatically contrasting with her navy-blue jacket.

Gracie glanced down at her own outfit: a warm white

turtleneck over loose, flowered pants. Not so bad, she thought, for a couple of pillars of the community.

"A toast!" Rocky Gravino, the owner and editor of the *Mason County Gazette,* raised his glass. "To our very own Gracie Parks. Best darned cook in all of Indiana. No . . . " He shifted his burly figure in his seat. "Make that the entire U.S. of A!"

Everyone laughed, rose to their feet and drank a toast to their hostess.

Gracie motioned to them to sit back down. "Thank you, dear friends. I'm so glad you managed to come on a night like tonight and join Uncle Miltie and me." She smiled at her uncle, who had managed to sneak an extra helping of rice before rising. "I know Thanksgiving's over, but I'm still feeling truly grateful. Not everyone is so blessed."

"You're so right," Paul said. His eyes shone. "This is a difficult time of year for many who are less fortunate."

Marge nodded, her silver bell earrings tinkling softly. "And it just gets tougher, what with the Christmas season approaching. I see lots of sad people walk by the shop. You can just tell that they're down on their luck." She looked at her plate. "I wish there was something we could do, something more *personal.* You know, beyond what we participate in through the church."

Everyone was silent for a minute. Gracie eyed the array of

delicious food spread out on the table, breathed in the warmth of her well-furnished home and felt a twinge of guilt. She was truly fortunate! And that advantage, she knew with certainty, was due mainly to the Lord's grace. "Marge is right. We don't always know where our offerings go. Perhaps there's something we *can* do for some of our own."

Pastor Paul glowed with enthusiasm. "Yes! Yes! Of course, many of our needy fellow citizens are receiving some sort of help already . . . but then others remain. Ones who aren't so lucky, who may not make their needs as public." His eyes swept the table. "When I see all this food . . . I want to imagine others sharing a similar delicious bounty." He hesitated. "Why, that's it!"

All eyes were on the young unmarried pastor. "In the past, I know there were years when a local family was sponsored for Christmas. Dare we stretch ourselves and resources a little further? Perhaps a hamper of food, maybe some gifts?

"But time is short. To make it work in the best possible way—to make a real difference—takes money! Everyone's starting to get so busy and distracted!"

"Selling chocolate's a good fund-raiser at this time of year," Uncle Miltie interjected, his gaze straying to the lemon meringue pie on the sideboard. "Folks always want something sweet at the ready for unexpected guests or to take as a present."

Will wonders never cease! Gracie thought, staring at her

uncle. Since when did he become Mr. Manners? Then, she followed his eyes as they focused on the pie and understood. She smiled inside. As the others tossed around some more ideas, she started clearing the table. Rocky was at her side in a minute, several plates in his large hands. "Sure was a great meal, Gracie! You really *are* the best, no exaggerating."

She blushed slightly, knowing how her meals pleased him. "You know how I love cooking," she said, leading him into the kitchen. "Especially for dear friends." She paused, and decided to take the opportunity. "Rocky? There's something I've been wanting to mention. I think there's room in the paper for more coverage of the local art scene. There's lots of news and sports, of course, but . . . well, you might be falling down a little on the job in other areas. . . ."

Rocky eyed her carefully. "Why, Mrs. Parks! I never knew you were a patron of the arts."

"Oh, Mr. Gravino," Gracie teased, "there's a lot you don't know about me."

"I'll bet." He wiped his hands on a dish towel. "It's not a bad suggestion though. What were you thinking?"

She frowned. "I'm not really sure. Maybe a regular feature, emphasizing the human interest angle. Introducing some of the creatively inclined people in and around Willow Bend."

His blue eyes twinkled. "Any Picasso in particular?"

"Well, I'm sure there are many, but I have recently met one. Florence Jackson, a potter. She's very talented. She's recently widowed and struggling to adapt. A little recognition would really help."

"What's going on in there?" Uncle Miltie shouted from the dining room. "The meringue's starting to melt."

"Maybe I'll interview her myself," Rocky told her. "Your endorsement counts for a lot with me, you know."

"Thanks! That'd be great. Now, we'd better get in there before Uncle Miltie takes the slicing into his own hands. If you'll just carry these," she added, handing him a pile of dessert plates, "I'll bring the coffee and tea."

They returned to find that Paul had cleared the rest of the table while Marge had set the pie in front of Gracie's place.

Gracie was about to cut the first piece when she suddenly noticed the colorful platter underneath it. "What's this?" Carefully lifting the lemon pie, she was rewarded with the sight of an uneven ceramic plate with thick edges. The pattern decorating it was a childlike, spiralling crimson rose design. She glanced around the table. Marge shook her head, Rocky put a finger to his lips and Paul just grinned.

Uncle Miltie cleared his throat.

Putting the dish to one side, she stared at him. "You made this?" Her uncle tried to look modest. Gracie glanced again at the uneven edges. "Why, Uncle Miltie, it's . . . it's beautiful!" Gracie exclaimed, jumping up and giving him a kiss. "It's a rose, isn't it?"

"The Rose of Sharon, " he replied, beaming with pleasure.

"From the Song of Solomon," Pastor Paul said softly. "'I am the Rose of Sharon and the lily of the valley,'" he quoted.

"Uncle Miltie, you made that?" Marge remained incredulous.

"Yup. Learning to be a potter."

"Good for you," Paul said, as Marge patted Uncle Miltie's hand in congratulations.

"Will you make one for me?" Marge asked. "I'm particularly fond of willow trees, especially in the winter." She smiled at the questioning faces. "Isaiah called it 'the Spirit of Spring.'"

Paul smiled. "A good choice. There are willows growing throughout the Holy Land, but their leaves and color differs from ours."

"I'd be glad to find you a picture," Marge assured Gracie's uncle.

He gave her a pleased thumbs-up.

"Why don't you make a few for sale?" Paul suggested. "Maybe help raise a bit of money for our family?"

"*Hmm*," Uncle Miltie thought aloud. He considered the idea for a moment. "I could even use the flowers of the Bible as a theme."

"Wonderful!" Gracie said, returning to her chair. She ran her finger over the pattern. It *was* beautiful, she thought. And not just in the eye of the beholder. "This is too precious to hide under a cake or pie," Gracie said. "I'm going to get a stand and put it on the sideboard, for all to see."

"Speaking of pie," her uncle reminded her.

Gracie grinned and reached for the knife.

Soon, they were devouring large wedges and stirring their mugs. "This takes the cake," Paul said, licking his fork. "Or should I say 'pie'?"

Everyone laughed. Rocky swallowed a last bit of meringue. "Too bad you couldn't sell this dessert," he declared. "You'd make a fortune." But then he added, "Of course you do sell them when they're part of one of your catering jobs."

Gracie cocked her head. "How about a pie bee?" she inquired.

Marge turned toward her. Rocky's fork, newly reloaded, stopped midway to his mouth. "A what?"

"A pie-making bee," Gracie explained. "The choir could get together, bake and freeze as many pies as they can and then sell them, perhaps after service one Sunday. We did it once, several years ago."

"That's a great idea, Gracie," Marge said, stirring her tea. "It was a lot of fun. How about selling them at the Christmas pageant? Everyone loves homemade pie!"

"This annual celebration of our Lord's birth really is one of my favorite events on the church calendar." Paul said. "The

Sunday school kids, bless their tiny hearts, reenact the miracle of the first Christmas."

Marge nodded. "It's really very cute. Some teeny, tiny boy or girl always forgets his or her line, starts crying and then the others rush over to help out." She laughed indulgently. "Sometimes, the play never finishes. But no one minds."

"Last year, one of the wise men almost sat on the Christ Child," Uncle Miltie said. "Made a heck of a racket."

Rocky's eyebrows rose.

"It was Susie Frantz's baby."

"We've got a ceramic infant this year," Paul added quickly, seeing the grin spreading across Rocky's rugged features. "

"We're the angels," said Marge. "A heavenly choir singing the new babe's praises."

"You know, Rocky, how you always find it charming when you do stop by." Gracie reminded him, knowing how reluctant he could be when it came to religious ritual. And when he wasn't reluctant, he was unpredictable. It was an area where they'd long ago agreed to disagree.

He smiled broadly at her. "Stop by?" He gestured at his empty plate. "You serve me another piece of this pie and I'll even play the part of the donkey!"

WELL, GOOD NIGHT, GRACIE," Rocky said, pausing by the front door. "Thanks—your ability to come up with new definitions of 'delicious,' no matter how many times you've fed me, well, it's almost one for the record books!"

He turned to his companion. "Ready, Paul?"

The pastor tugged a knit cap over his ears, shivered, then gave a thumbs-up. "I really appreciate the lift, Rocky. The sidewalks look a lot more treacherous than when I came."

"I'm off too," Marge declared, swirling a purple tasseled scarf around her neck. She gave Uncle Miltie and Gracie a quick hug. "Big yum! I ate too much, but don't I always? Diets can always start tomorrow . . . and I'm not saying *which* tomorrow."

"Need a lift?" Rocky asked. "Or are you going to roll on home on your own?"

Marge grinned. "Think I can manage it, thanks."

He held out an arm. "May I at least escort you?"

Marge laughed and accepted his offer. "Not one but two gentlemen at my elbow. Paul, you take the left one, and, Rocky, you may have the right."

With the door opened, they all shivered as a gust of bitterly cold air snaked inside, trailing snow. Gracie waved goodbye and watched as her friends navigated her front steps and stepped through half a foot of newly-fallen snow. Rocky began clearing his small black sedan while Paul guided Marge toward her front door. He waited until Marge had stepped inside before heading back to join Rocky.

At that moment, Gooseberry pounded up Gracie's steps, just making it in before she shut out the icy air once again. As she turned, she heard Uncle Miltie whistling in the dining room. "Be right there!" she called, knowing he'd not refuse her help with the clean-up.

"Cup of tea?" Uncle Miltie asked half an hour later as Gracie poured out more catfood and filled Gooseberry's bowl with fresh water. The no-longer damp cat yawned and stretched, now perched atop the refrigerator, one of his favorite vantage points. Dropping down at the clatter of food hitting dish, he made for his meal with haughty grace.

"Oh, you're a dear. I'd love tea," Gracie replied. She pushed the button to start the dishwasher.

The doorbell rang.

Gracie glanced at her watch: 8:40 P.M.

"Who could *that* be at this hour?" Uncle Miltie asked, tugging a pair of teabags from Gracie's old ironstone sugar bowl.

"I'll get it," Gracie said, stepping into the hallway.

"Betcha it's Marge," Uncle Miltie's voice floated after her. "Forgot her lipstick or some such thing."

Gracie pulled open the door with a grin. "What'd you forget?"

"Excuse me?" a boy's voice replied.

Surprised, Gracie looked down. A teenager dressed in a duffle jacket and wool cap stood looking politely at Gracie. "Hello," Gracie said. "May I help you?"

The boy smiled shyly and gestured with a shovel. "I was hoping to help you, ma'am."

"Oh."

The boy waited.

"Do I know you?" Gracie asked, peering closely at the freckled face.

He shrugged. "Don't think so." He turned, pointing to her walkway. "Would you like me to shovel your walk for five dollars?"

Gracie was about to say that it didn't need clearing when she realized that her walk again was nestled under several inches of new snow.

"Did you say five dollars?"

He nodded.

"That seems fair," she replied. "Do you want the money now?"

"Nope." A grin crushed his freckles. "I know where you live."

Gracie smiled. "What's your name?"

"Trent, ma'am. Trent Freeman. I'll knock when I'm finished," he added, closing the door.

"Tea's ready," Uncle Miltie called.

As she returned to the kitchen, he asked, "Who was that?"

Gracie gratefully took her mug and slumped into a chair. Taking a sip, she sighed happily and replied, "A young angel named Trent Freeman. He's going to clear the walk. I don't think I could have faced another round with a shovel." She swallowed more tea and leaned back. "Not tonight."

"Sure wish I could help you," her uncle said. He clenched his hands. "But my strength's not up to shoveling, and, come winter, that means I'm pretty useless."

"Nonsense!" She reached across the table to touch him. "Aren't these the artistic fingers that created my wonderful Rose of Sharon platter?"

He laughed. "I'm glad it pleased you, Gracie dear. You sure please me. Guess I'll catch the news then," he said. "Find out if this blizzard's ever going to end."

Gooseberry now leapt into his mistress's lap, circling until he found a comfortable position, at which point he began cleaning his paws. Stroking him lightly, Gracie slowly finished her tea and enjoyed the moment of quiet.

Twenty minutes later, the doorbell rang again. Gooseberry started and, rousing himself, streaked into the living room. As Gracie went into the hall, she saw him pounce on her sofa, pad along the top, then plop down into his preferred seat by the window.

"All finished?" she asked, pulling open the door.

Trent shook his head and body, showering her step with snowflakes. He shifted from foot to foot, obviously cold. "Yes, ma'am."

The walk was cleared down to the paving stones. "You've done a fine job, thank you. Come in and get warm while I get you the money."

As they entered the house, she noticed the boy's nostrils flare. "Hungry?"

Trent nodded shyly.

"How about some homemade lemon meringue pie and a hot chocolate? Do you have the time? It's getting late."

This time his nod was eager.

"Hang up your hat and coat in there, please," Gracie instructed, showing him the hall closet. "And follow me." As they passed the entrance to the living room, Gracie paused. "Uncle Miltie, this is Trent Freeman."

The boy hesitated. For a moment, he seemed to stare at the older man. "Pleased to meet you, sir," he finally said.

Uncle Miltie nodded.

"In here," Gracie said, offering Trent a kitchen chair. "The hot chocolate will take a couple of minutes, but the pie's ready." She reached into the fridge and pulled out the remaining pie and a bottle of milk. She filled a mug, popped it into the microwave and punched a couple of buttons. Then she cut a generous slice of pie and handed it, along with a fork, to Trent. He was slim, she noticed, about thirteen or fourteen years of age with fine features, light brown hair and matching eyes. His jeans were wet and dirty and his 'Fish or Die!' sweatshirt was wrinkled.

"Tell me a bit about yourself," she asked, joining him at the table. "You like fishing?"

For a moment, he looked puzzled until she pointed to his sweatshirt. Trent grinned while he attacked his pie. He ate ravenously.

"Do you live nearby?"

He swallowed and shook his head. "On a farm. Off Hollow Hill Road. This is awesome! Haven't had homemade pie in a . . ." He hesitated, then stabbed another double-sized bite.

His plate was empty by the time the microwave beeped. Gracie got up and made the hot chocolate. "Marshmallows?"

She noticed a bluish line beneath the boy's eyes and wondered if he was getting enough sleep. He nodded an eager assent.

"Do your parents know where you are?" she asked,

handing over the steaming mug, the miniature marshmallows bobbing on the surface.

He nodded, sipping gingerly.

Gracie glanced at the kitchen clock. "Are you sure you don't need to call them?"

"Naaa, nobody ther—uh . . . no, thank you." He stared into his hot chocolate intently, as if the marshmallows might have a message to impart before melting.

"Freeman," Gracie said. "Not a very common name. I met a young girl today named Bridget Freeman. Is she your sister, by any chance?"

Trent's eyelashes flickered.

"She's very pretty."

Trent rolled his eyes. "Sure works at it hard enough."

Gracie swallowed a smile. "Have you other brothers or sisters?"

"Another sister, Trixie," he said, barely containing his disdain. He shivered. "Surrounded by girls."

"Your father must love it."

Trent frowned and gulped his drink. "He's gone."

"Oh! I'm so sorry," Gracie replied. "You poor thing. To lose a father so young."

Trent's eyes widened. "*He* didn't die," he said, a note of contempt slipping into his voice. "Just took off."

Gracie didn't know what to say. She was startled, not only by the boy's statement and tone, but by the odd emphasis placed on the pronoun *he*. She waited for a couple of moments. "Would you like another piece of pie?"

"Yes, thank you! Please!"

As she cut the second wedge, she asked cautiously, "How's your mom doing?"

Trent was silent for a full minute. When he spoke, it was in a whisper. "She died. Last year."

Gracie's heart twisted at the pain she saw cross the boy's face. She could barely resist the urge to rush over and hug his thin shoulders. "Oh, Trent," she managed to say as she handed him the plate. "I'm so sorry." She couldn't imagine what it was like to lose both your parents at such a young age. A tragedy of that magnitude had to take an awful toll. She watched him carefully.

He shook himself, as though to push away any sad thoughts before they could attach themselves. He cut into the fresh dessert. "We're doing all right," he replied, his voice almost too cheerful. "My aunt came to take care of us." He swallowed. "She's really great, loves to cook. Now we have a freezer full of stuff—meat, fruit, all kinds of food." He stared at Gracie, dark eyes suddenly defiant. "We're doing just fine."

"I'm glad," Gracie said, as he finished the pie. "What's your aunt's name?

"Harriet . . . Harriet Kimball," he said, eyes lowered.

Gracie stood, grabbed her purse from the counter and

fished out a five dollar bill. Handing it to him, she said, "Do you feel game for a bit more shoveling?"

Trent's face fell.

"I don't think I can get the car out of the driveway to give you a lift home."

Stuffing the bill into his pocket, he shook his head. He headed out of the kitchen toward the front hall. "You don't need to. I'm, uh, meeting my aunt."

"Where? At least I can give you a lift there."

Trent shoved his feet into his boots and pulled on his jacket and cap. "No, no thank you," he replied quickly. "It's not far from here. I can walk."

Gracie eyed him doubtfully. "You sure?"

Trent was out the door as an answer.

"Nice meeting you!" Gracie shouted at his back. As she watched the slight silhouette charge through the snow, she wondered, why the sudden rush? The boy had seemed fairly comfortable until she had offered him a ride home. Why would that be so disturbing?

Because it probably wasn't, she chided herself, returning to the kitchen. He's just a teenager. She chuckled, remembering her own son, Arlen, at that age. Tall, gawky, half of him wanting to be hugged, the other half pushing her away. Thinking it over, Gracie realized that Trent Freeman just seemed to be a pretty typical teenager. A few mood swings were all part of the package. It was a blessing, really, considering what he'd been through.

A CRIMSON TINT slowly splintered the dawn sky. Bundled in her winter walking clothes, Gracie tramped slowly and cautiously through the uncleared sidewalks of her neighbourhood, enjoying the squeak her boots created in the snow. Though the Saturday morning air bit at her exposed face and threatened to invade her heavy gloves, she was enjoying herself.

After the first snowfall, Willow Bend always looked so different—a tableau of sparkling crystals and dazzling light. The jagged panorama of buildings, trees and criss-crossing roads huddled beneath a soft blanket, contrasts blunted, edges and angles blurred. It was like entering an alien—yet tantalizingly familiar—world.

Gracie had always loved Indiana's distinctive four seasons and, unlike several of her friends, eagerly anticipated the annual quarterly transitions. *Dear Lord, Your beloved earth, so much a symbol of Your love, fills me with hope no matter whether it's green with spring, orange and yellow in autumn, or dazzlingly white as it is this blessed morning. I am at one with You and with this gorgeous landscape. Even a walk in air so frosty that it burns is a pleasure, for I know that it is You Who guides my every step.*

Invigorated by the effort of breaking a trail in this muted and transformed landscape, she softly sang the words to *Victory in Jesus,* one of her favorite hymns, and began planning her day. Rounding the last corner en route home, she noticed a large pick-up truck equipped with a slanted plow expertly clearing the last chunks of snow from her driveway. Heading across the road, she waited until the driver, Harry Durant, saw her. He grinned, put the truck into park and rolled down his partially frosted window.

"Good morning, Gracie," the garage owner said, his voice creating a tiny cloud of condensation. She caught a whiff of diesel fumes, Harry's usual cologne. "Almost missed you. Well, what do you think of it?"

Gracie blinked, then followed his outstretched arm toward the clean driveway. "Oh! Wonderful, Harry. Just wonderful! It would have taken me ages to shovel out from under that. Been here very long?"

Harry tugged at his wool cap, then slapped the steering wheel. "No more than ten minutes with this baby."

"Well, I'm very grateful," Gracie replied, looking at the

mounds of snow lining her drive. "Have you a minute? I've got a partial payment."

"You don't owe me anything really, Gracie," he said. "My freezer's still bulging with your last installment." He paused, squinting. "Why? What's on offer?"

"Freshly baked lemon meringue pie." She watched his eyes light up.

"Well, it doesn't seem right to refuse, seeing how you've gone to all the trouble of making it." He scratched his grizzled chin. "How about we call it an advance on the next storm, okay?"

She smiled, slipped inside and removed the last of the pie from the refrigerator and wrapped it in foil. "I've still got a load of driveways ahead of me," he said, licking his lips. "This may not make it home." He tipped his cap. "Much obliged, Gracie."

Closing the door behind him, Gracie was greeted by a note on the kitchen table from her uncle stating that he would return by mid-afternoon. She showered and, while eating lunch, began to draft a tentative list of the necessary ingredients. Using the church's petty cash, she would purchase shortening, flour, sugar, seasonings and extra pie plates. For the various fillings she was counting on her fellow choir members. With a half-finished cup of tea in her hand, she began calling them.

"Hello, Barb?"

Someone sneezed on the other end of the phone line.

"Bless you. Barb, is that you?"

"Hi, Gracie," replied the muffled voice belonging to Eternal Hope's organist and choir director. "I've got a cold, as you can hear." Barb Jennings sneezed again. "It's the sudden change in weather."

"Oh, you poor dear," Gracie said. "Well, I'm sorry to bother you. Would you like me to call later?"

"No, it's all right," Barb's voice rose slightly. "Are you worried about tomorrow's selection? Has someone complained? We can still make a change."

For a moment, Gracie didn't understand. "Oh, no. Not at all. I like the hymns you've chosen. So does everyone else."

She heard Barb sigh with relief. Poor thing, Gracie thought. Always so hard on herself, and tending to perfectionism. As assistant choir director, Gracie tried her best to bolster her friend's confidence. Despite being a superb pianist and an experienced and admired choir director, Barb Jennings sometimes seemed her own worst enemy. Given to self-doubt and second-guessing, the talented musician found it very difficult to relax and enjoy her beloved avocation.

"I'm calling for a very different reason. A couple of us were talking over dinner last night and ..."

"Only your cooking could have gotten people out in that storm, Gracie," Barb teased.

"It was our remembering Thanksgiving that prompted the

idea. How it reminds us we're so fortunate while many others aren't. I know we already do a lot of charitable work, but would you like to be involved in something more personal?"

"Like what?" Barb was curious.

"Well, what about raising some money and using it to sponsor a local needy family? That way, we can experience a real sense of accomplishment."

Barb blew her nose. "It sounds good, Gracie, but you're right, we already host a number of events to raise money for different charities. What would be different about this?"

"Well," Gracie replied. "First and most importantly, the funds would go *directly* to a deserving family in our very own area. And secondly, I thought we might try another pie-making bee." She paused, to let the idea sink in. "Remember the last one? It was a big hit."

There was a long pause. Gracie could hear her friend's audible breathing. Poor thing!

Finally, Barb said, "Well, why not?" She paused again. "Will you want me to be in charge of pastry?" Despite Barb's cold, Gracie could hear the pride in her voice.

"Of course!" Gracie replied. "I was hoping you'd offer. No one makes a flakier crust."

Barb gave a little pleased grunt. "When?"

"*Hmm* . . . that's a good question. I was thinking about a week from today. That way we'll take care of it before the Christmas rush."

Next Gracie dialed the number for one of the tenors, Rick Harding. His wife, Comfort, answered on the third ring.

"Rick's outside," Comfort told her. "He's making a snow family for Lillian." She chuckled. "I'm watching from the window. He's been out there for ages and he's *just* putting the heads on. I had to bring her in. She was freezing to death." Gracie heard the delightful sounds of the toddler's laughter. "Hold on. Here he comes."

A moment later, Rick's smooth voice filled her ear. He was, in fact, the choir's best tenor. "Hello, Gracie? Your timing's perfect. I don't have any coal. Any ideas for my snow people's eyes?"

Gracie contemplated her kitchen, finally noticing the old ironstone sugar bowl where she stored her favorite orange pekoe tea. "In a pinch, I'd try wet teabags. It's so cold, they'd probably freeze before they dried out."

Rick laughed heartily. "Leave it to you to think of some-thing that simple. Thanks! Now, were you looking for a snow cat for your front yard, to keep Gooseberry company, or is there something else I can do for you?"

It was Gracie's turn to laugh. Then she told him about the pie-making bee. As she'd hoped, he immediately agreed to participate.

"A couple of things," he added. "I'm as good with pastry as I am at making snowmen. That's the crew for me. None of this slicing and dicing!"

"No problem. I could use your strong hands preparing the dough. What's your other problem?"

"I'm on call for EMT next weekend so I might have to dash out."

Gracie assured him that his duties as a volunteer emergency medical technician superceded those of a pastry chef. Then she asked him which fillings he'd take responsibility for bringing.

"Count me in for pecans. Should be able to bring a couple of pounds, maybe more. I'll offer the brown sugar, too."

"Splendid," Gracie said. She heard another voice.

"Uh, Gracie? Comfort would like to help out. She'd need to bring Lillian along. Would that be all right?"

"That'd be wonderful! Well, I've got to make some more calls. See you tomorrow."

Then Gracie tried Don Delano's number but had to leave a message on his machine. The same thing happened when she called Estelle Livett and Lester Twomley. By now, she had her message down pat and was about to leave it after dialing the Anderson residence when Tyne picked up. Gracie was glad because this saved her another phone call. Anything she told Tyne, she knew would be passed on to her twin sister, Tish, within the hour.

"Oh, we loved the last one!" Tyne said, after hearing Gracie's pitch. "Count us in." Gracie smiled at how she automatically agreed for the both of them. "What can we bring?"

"Have you used up all of your husband's rhubarb?"

Tyne laughed. "I wish! You know farmer John. He can't grow enough of the stuff. Both Tish and my freezers are pink when you open them. Could you use some?"

"Four or five pounds would be a blessing from heaven."

"Consider it done. Anything else?"

"Just give John my regards. See you tomorrow."

With a contented sigh, Gracie replaced the receiver and scribbled on her ingredients list. Then, in the midst of ringing Marybeth Bower's number, a thought interrupted her. Digging out her local phone book, Gracie found Trent Freeman's number and dialed it. He'd said his aunt kept a full freezer, so perhaps she had a few pounds of fruit to spare.

An answering machine responded. Gracie listened to the voice, so muffled it was unrecognizable, and left her message. She dialed Marybeth's and recited the same message. As she was making herself a light lunch, the phone rang.

"What's going on? I've been calling home for ages but couldn't get through!" Uncle Miltie shouted.

Taken aback by his tone, Gracie replied, "I'm sorry, but I've been making arrangements for the pie bee."

"Forget the darned pie bee," he commanded. "Come right down to the senior center! Now! You're not going to believe what's happened."

"What's the matter? More jewelry missing?"

There was no answer. Gracie realized her uncle had hung up.

In a bit of a panic, she dragged on her coat and boots and headed out to Fannie Mae. As she navigated carefully through the newly plowed streets of Willow Bend, she could only wonder, what had happened to cause her own dessert-loving uncle to put anything at all ahead of pie?

6

DESPITE THE EFFORTS of the local road crews, it wasn't a day for making speedy progress across Willow Bend, and Gracie had barely reached the door of the senior center when her uncle threw it open for her. He had been waiting with mounting agitation.

"Gracie," he said with relief. "You don't know how glad I am to see you." He turned to reveal Florence Jackson standing behind him.

"Hi, Gracie," she said. Her cheeks were bright pink, but it wasn't from the cold.

"Gracie!" Molly Cook's voice rose above the others. She strode over. "Do you know anything about this nasty business?"

Gracie took a deep breath and replied slowly. "Please just tell me what's going on. Is anyone hurt?"

"Follow me!" Her uncle demanded. With his walker clacking the floor as if for emphasis, he began marching down the hall.

"No one's hurt," Molly whispered as the three women followed Uncle Miltie. "It's just . . . well, something *very* unpleasant." She lowered her voice even further. Gracie had to strain to hear her next words. "I don't want the others to know."

"Know what?" Gracie asked. "Will somebody let me in on what's going on?"

No one replied. Gracie realized that her uncle had disappeared into the kiln room. Molly quickly closed the door behind them.

Gracie glanced quickly around. The long tables were still cluttered with pots, bowls and small figurines, some partially painted, others still the reddish-brown of unfired clay. Gracie noticed a row of freshly painted farm animals, obviously part of several Nativity scenes. She couldn't see anything out of place. Puzzled, she waited for an explanation. In a dramatic gesture, Uncle Miltie swept his hand downward. Her eyes followed his crooked index finger to the floor.

Gracie gasped.

All she saw were smashed bits of ceramic. Dozens of

pieces, of different sizes and shapes, lay strewn everywhere in a jumble of colors and glazes.

"Someone must not want me here," Flo said, her voice catching. "But who? I really don't understand. None of it's truly valuable, except to me—but they're like pieces of myself."

"Uh . . ." Uncle Miltie started hesitantly, gazing sadly at the fragments. "I'm not sure it's . . ."

"Whoever did this," Molly interrupted, "will be punished! I will not tolerate wanton damage of any kind. No matter what the reason."

As Gracie eyed the broken bits, an odd thought hit her. If the act of breaking the pottery hadn't been so violent, the colorful mosaic results would have been almost beautiful. She reached down and gently picked up a large piece, painted and glazed a brilliant white. After a moment, she realized that it was a partial wing. Carefully stepping across the tiles, she bent again. This time, the cracked bit stared back at her. It was a single baby-blue eye. Then she noticed other pieces, some white, some fired and unpainted, but all with an identical rounded edge and curved line. Many more blue eyes glared up at her. A golden circle glinted in the light. She rubbed it carefully, recognizing it to be a incomplete halo. There were several more at her feet.

She turned to the others. "Why, these are all . . ."

"Angels," said her uncle, nodding. "That's right."

"What do you mean?" Flo and Molly asked as one.

Uncle Miltie looked a bit sheepish. "I . . . I tried to tell you earlier, Flo, but, you . . ." he shrugged. "Anyway, I think they're mine, not Flo's pieces. If she hadn't been so upset, she would have seen it wasn't her work that was harmed." His voice hardened. "Someone deliberately smashed my guardian angels."

"*Your* guardian angels?" This time it was Gracie who spoke along with Flo.

Her uncle blushed. "I was making them as presents." He handed Gracie a flimsy, sculpted piece of rubber. "It was my first time using a mold." He held it up.

She could see that the mold had a clear outline of a angel, whose wings, halo and deep-set eyes were identical to the remnants in her hands.

Uncle Miltie reached down for a chalk-colored scrap. "I hadn't finished painting them all." He sighed. "It was a lot of work."

Flo spread out her arms. "You're sure that these are all your angels?"

"Pretty sure," Uncle Miltie answered. "Have you checked your pieces? I had a quick look, but I don't think anything else is missing."

While Flo moved about the room, peeking underneath cloths that covered odd shapes, and examined the open shelves, Molly grabbed a broom. "You don't mind, Uncle

Miltie?" she asked. He slowly shook his head. Gracie found another broom behind the kiln and joined her.

"Why would anyone do such a terrible thing?" Molly asked, pushing shards out from under a table. "What could they possibly gain?"

"Looks like the work of a madman," said Flo. "Or someone with a violent temper."

"What else is broken besides my uncle's angels?" Gracie asked Flo.

The potter shook her head. "All my work is present and accounted for, I guess." She glanced at the various pieces scattered about the table tops. "I'm not exactly sure, but I don't think anything else is missing."

Uncle Miltie ran his fingers through his thick gray hair. "Why would someone ruin *only* my angels?"

Molly picked up a purple and gold figurine of one of the three wise men and studied for a moment. "Could it be a message of some sort? The center's for all seniors, independent of religion, but maybe someone doesn't like Christmas."

Gracie raised her eyebrows. "Yes, but then the Nativity figures would have been damaged, as well."

She glanced at Florence. "Have you any enemies in Willow Bend? It's hard to believe Uncle Miltie does, unless it's an anti-bad-joke-minded citizen."

Flo sank onto a stool. "I know Molly had some other complaints," she admitted.

The administrator nodded. "They were pretty minor, really. Just that a couple of people didn't like the smell. We increased the ventilation and now fire the kiln later in the day." She made a wiping motion with her hands. "That seemed to do it."

Gracie eyed her uncle as he watched Molly dump the last chunks of pottery into the garbage bin. The elderly man's shoulders were slumped, his earlier anger dissipated. "What about you, Uncle Miltie?" Gracie asked carefully. "You beaten anybody lately at pinochle? I was just teasing about the bad jokes."

He smiled and shook his head.

"This is awful," Molly said. "We still haven't found Mrs. Simmons's bracelet and now this . . . this malicious destruction!" She paused, as though considering an unpleasant decision. "I'm going to have to call Herb Bower." She grimaced. "It looks like we've got another mystery on our hands."

7

LATER THAT AFTERNOON, Gracie finished grating a chunk of cheddar, then walked over to stir a large pot of bubbling chili. Uncle Miltie set the last utensil on the kitchen table and stopped to scratch Gooseberry's ears. The big cat was draped across the seat of one of the kitchen chairs. He sniffed delicately, scrunched up his pink nose and proceeded to stretch to clean his striped back. Uncle Miltie chuckled.

"Smells mighty good. You sure that's got no meat in it?"

Gracie smiled. "It's completely vegetarian," she replied, dipping a large spoon into the crock pot. "Want a taste?"

"Sure." He sipped the spoonful cautiously. "Oww! It's hot."

Gracie held up a shaker of hot peppers. "Hot as in *warm*, or hot as in *spicy*?"

"Both." Her uncle ran his tongue along his upper lip.

"Too spicy?"

"Give me a minute," he replied. "I need to wait until my taste buds stop begging for mercy. Can't you hear them?"

She brandished the shaker at him.

He held his hands up in mock defeat. "Really, it's great. You'd never know it lacked meat." He turned to the bread-board where a loaf of whole-wheat bread sat cooling. "One lump or two?" he asked, reaching for the serrated knife.

"One," she replied. "Would you mind watching the stove? I just want to make a quick call." Her uncle nodded as Gracie picked up the phone and dialed the Freeman's number. She sat down, listening to the rings.

Finally, a child answered.

"Hello? Is Harriet Kimball there?"

"No," the small voice said.

"Oh, you must be Trixie," Gracie said. "Hello, dear. I know your brother and sister. May I speak to one of them?"

"No."

"Oh. *Uhmm* . . . are they nearby?"

"No."

This is ridiculous, Gracie thought, standing. "Are you *sure* one of them can't come to the phone? I'd like to speak to them. Tell Trent it's Mrs. Parks. And, *please*, don't just say no this time."

The little girl didn't. Instead, she hung up.

"Well, for heaven's sake—"

With one hand vigorously stirring the pot, her uncle looked quizzically at her.

The phone rang again.

"Oh, that'll be Trent," Gracie said, picking up the receiver. "Hello, Trent? You really should teach your little sis—"

"Gracie? It's Herb."

"Oh, I'm so sorry, Herb! I thought you were someone else."

"Evidently. You're obviously waiting for a call. When's a convenient time to phone you back?"

"It's all right, Herb." Gracie slid back into her seat. "Now's fine. I'm just giving us dinner. What can I do for you?"

"Sorry to trouble you," Willow Bend's police chief replied. "But I'm just checking some facts about my mother-in-law's missing bracelet. You were there when she discovered it was gone?"

Gracie leaned in her chair and nodded to her uncle as he began slicing a thick piece of bread. "Well, Uncle Miltie was giving me a tour of the kiln room—he's taken up pottery— when we heard a yell. We ran out into the common room and your mother-in-law was almost hysterical. She was con- vinced her bracelet had been stolen."

"It's not a new problem, unfortunately," said Herb. "I've offered to have the clasp fixed 'til I'm blue in the face. But she just won't let it out of her sight." Herb sighed heavily. "At least, not deliberately. You know she's lost it before?"

"Uh huh. Molly told me. Is that what you think happened this time?"

"I don't rightly know, to be honest. It hasn't been found yet, so it's possible. I'm still hoping it'll turn up stuck to some curtain or something, but Molly's asked me to check the premises on the off-chance I'll see what she hasn't. Libby's been driving us both crazy, phoning the house and the station practically every five minutes to see if it's been found. I do understand it's hard not to obsess about losing things when one's older—it's only that it's not the first time. Or the last."

He paused. "Oh, and before I forget, I understand you saw those broken ceramic pieces?"

"Yes. I felt sick, just looking at all that work of Uncle Miltie's down the drain."

"Might it have been a practical joke?"

"Not a very nice one, Herb."

"No, but usually they aren't, are they?"

"I suppose you're right." Gracie sighed. "Do you find it odd that the vandal only targeted Uncle Miltie's angels?"

"Yeah. Maybe." Another chuckle. "Your uncle been cheating at cards again?"

"Be serious, Herb. You don't think there's a deeper meaning to this . . . this willful destruction, do you?"

"How do you mean?"

"Well, it seems wicked somehow. The deliberate smashing

of *angels* worries me. As if it has some deeper meaning."

Herb didn't answer for a moment. "Guess so, Gracie, but honestly, I think that's a bit of a stretch. I don't have any theory I want to go with, but I think it must be some bad egg with a gripe we'll learn about soon enough. Even Willow Bend has its share. Hey, you said Uncle Miltie was right there?"

Gracie said yes, gesturing to her uncle.

"Mind if I speak with him for a moment?"

"Not at all. Just a moment, I'll put him on."

"Oh, before you go. Marybeth says she's prepared to raid the Willow Mart for every remaining can of pumpkin filling on the shelves—whatever that means."

Gracie laughed. "Thanks. Give her my regards."

Uncle Miltie took the phone. While she ladled the chili into bowls and buttered the bread, Gracie heard her uncle's replies. They were almost identical to her own, except that she heard him say that he was certain many members of the senior center knew that he was making the angels. She poured two glasses of water just as he hung up.

"We're ready."

Her uncle attacked his chili as though he hadn't eaten for a week. After a few minutes, he finally paused for breath. "Too spicy for you?" he asked, gesturing at her untouched meal.

"No. There's something . . . something bothering me. It's on the tip of my tongue, but I just can't put a name to it."

"A spoonful of this should stop it in its tracks." He halted, realizing his niece wasn't smiling. "Come on, dear. They were *my* angels that were destroyed. You've got to eat." He patted her arm affectionately. "After all, you're the only angel I have left."

HUGE DOWNY SNOWFLAKES swirled slowly then disappeared against the white vinyl siding of Eternal Hope Community Church. As Gracie carried in another box of supplies, her feet moved automatically along the curving snow path and into the first-floor kitchen, an addition to the century-old building. It was well-equipped and organized, having been designed by the women in the church three decades earlier. Her uncle was standing near the sink. "I've tried making an upside-down cake," he said. "Want to guess what happened?"

Pastor Paul hesitated. He had wandered in to fill a cup with coffee. "Okay, I'll bite. How'd it turn out?"

Uncle Miltie grinned. "It was a complete flop."

Both Gracie and the pastor groaned.

The week had flown by. Gracie had spent much of the time assisting Pat Allen in the church secretary's tiny office, located just off the sanctuary. Not surprisingly, the church correspondence and filing had been piling up since Pat had begun volunteering at the senior center.

At home, Gracie had come to depend on Trent Freeman. The early days of December had been accompanied by more bitter winds and blowing snow, and only with the young teenager's assistance could she keep her walk and driveway relatively passable. He had gone around to Marge's house, too, and also helped keep the sidewalk in front of her gift shop clear.

Gracie was unpacking the last box filled with shortening and sugar when she heard a car horn. Then another. Within minutes, Don Delano and Marge strolled in.

"Hello, everyone!" Don called, his wire-rimmed glasses suddenly fogging up. "Gracie, where do you want these?" He was carrying a stack of pie plates.

"In the sink. Yours, too, Marge."

Estelle Livett's strong soprano voice could be heard in the hall. Singing *Joy to the World*, she entered the kitchen. Marge and Don immediately joined in, Don's baritone voice contrasting nicely with the two women's blended tones.

The trio was about to launch into the third verse when Barb Jennings hustled in, her face dark with worry. "Sorry I'm late." The choir director handed four bags of frozen pitted cherries to Gracie. "Will these be all right?"

Gracie assured her they would be perfect, then glanced at her watch. Choir practice should always start on time so why not a pie bee? "Okay, the others will be here any minute. Might as well get started. Don? You game to peel and chop some pears?"

The science teacher saluted. Suddenly their minister reappeared.

"Can I help?" Paul asked, tying an apron around his black shirt.

"Marvelous! Thank you."

"What can I do?" Marge asked, sliding out of her heavy coat. She was already wearing a plastic apron with a design of shiny green and red holly.

"Well, I'd like you to roll pastry but for now, how about helping me set up some prep stations? Over there," she pointed to the sink, "is a good place to make the dough. We'll also need to use the big table for the rolling and the actual making of the pies. You're a dear, thanks. And, Estelle? I was thinking of using three or four people to roll dough."

"Sure," the stout woman replied. "I brought along those portable pastry boards you asked for." She tramped over to her coat, reached into her pockets and pulled out several rolls of heavy white plastic.

"What are they?" Lester Twomley asked as he walked in.

"See?" she said, nodding hello to Marybeth Bower. "It's a

non-sticky surface, and there's an outline in red providing the diameter of various pie sizes."

"An absolute marvel!" Marybeth said, hanging her coat on a hook at the back of the room. "Herb's mom gave me one last year. Don't know how I got the size right before without it. You just roll the dough until it roughly reaches the outline. Then, using a pie plate upside down, you can cut it to fit just right."

"Hey, gang!" Rick Harding shouted, wandering in with his pecan sacks. His daughter, her corn-rowed hair festooned with green and red ribbons, toddled along after, followed by Comfort, her mother, pushing a fold-up stroller.

The group next greeted the Turner twins, Tish and Tyne, who strolled in wearing matching down jackets and jeans. "We've got more apples," one said. "Two kinds," the other added. "They're tart, the best kind for pies, but we don't have to tell you that."

"Over here!" Don shouted, shoving peelings out of the way to make room.

"Well, I think we're all here," Gracie said. "Everyone else sends regrets."

"So, Gracie," Lester asked, rolling up his sleeves. "What now?"

"It's pretty simple, really," Gracie replied. "First, newcomers wash their hands, please."

As they obediently trooped to the sink, Gracie continued, "If you'll allow me, I've got it all worked out." They nodded. "We'll have an assembly line. Here are your assignments"— she dispatched her troops around the kitchen—"and, remember, we're making only medium pies. Questions, anyone? Oh, and, Comfort, jump in any chance you get, okay?"

The young woman nodded as she settled her daughter on her lap and began quietly reading *The Night Before Christmas*.

"Hey, Comfort," Les called, his hands deep in a large bowl. "Louder." Rick's wife smiled and strengthened her voice.

Rick quickly finished making his first ball of dough. Gracie tested it. "Perfect," she told him. "But I'm not surprised."

Rick grinned and tossed a kiss to his wife and daughter. He then broke the ball into three chunks, and handed a piece to Marge, Barb and Estelle. The trio went to work, deftly rolling the pastry, then carefully placing the bottom into a pie plate. Standing on the other side of the table, Gracie took the tops and laid them on a board farther up the assembly line. She then passed the plates to Marybeth, who, with a nod from Gracie, poured in a cup of the fruit mixture. Then Marybeth sprinkled in more of the mixture and a bit of cinnamon. Using a thick, black magic marker, Gracie now wrote "APPLE" across the first plastic bag and gave it to her uncle. Marybeth handed the pie plate to Tish, who carefully laid on the top layer of pastry. She pushed the pie across to her sister who expertly crimped the edges. Uncle Miltie then slid the completed dessert into its bag and tied it shut.

"One down!" he called.

The group cheered.

Concentrating carefully, the group worked steadily and produced another nine pies. By the time they had begun mixing the apple slices with pears, Estelle was humming again. Soon it would be time to switch gears and work on the pecans.

Barb tapped her rolling pin as though it were a baton. "How about a round of carols?"

There was a resounding cheer.

"Good!" Barb glanced at Uncle Miltie, Paul and Comfort. "You're all welcome to join in, okay? Right. Just like last Sunday, let's start off with *Good King Wenceslaus*."

"One of my favorites!" Marybeth declared.

The others continued with their assigned tasks and began singing. After the first verse, Barb banged her rolling pin again. "That was great! Now, for something a little more challenging . . . sopranos, sing the next verse while the rest continue with the first. Got it?"

Estelle, Marge and Marybeth broke into song. The others followed suit. The kitchen and nearby sanctuary were again filled with harmonizing voices, rising and falling, blending and separating beautifully until Lester's voice broke. "Uh oh," he whispered.

The soprano voices continued, but Don and Paul stared at their friend.

"What's wrong?" Don asked, as the women stopped singing.

Les stepped back from the counter. He brushed a lock of hair out of his eyes, leaving a trail of flour across his face. Gracie stifled a laugh. Lester stared into the large bowl in front of him. "Oh, I'm so sorry! I've lost count," he said, his eyes growing wide.

"Nobody needs to *count* to sing *Good King Wenceslaus*," Estelle snapped. "It's a simple four-four time."

Eyes downcast, Lester shook his head.

"The flour!" Rick cried. "You've lost count of the number of cups of flour!"

Lester's face turned as red as the frozen rhubarb.

For a moment, no one spoke. Then Barb chuckled nervously, triggering Marge and Don to laugh. Uncle Miltie slapped his thigh and roared from his belly.

"Don't worry, Les," Gracie said, moving quickly to his side. "No harm done. You've just got the dry ingredients there. You haven't added the shortening or the liquid part yet. You just have to start over."

"Did you hear the one about the guy who went to the doctor complaining that he couldn't stop stealing stamps?" Uncle Miltie began. "The doctor told him not to worry. That he would help him lick it."

Lester flicked a blob of dough in his direction. Uncle Miltie ducked and the dough hit Don's chest with a tiny splat.

"Hey!" The baritone grinned and tossed a handful of peelings toward Les.

"Hold it!" Gracie commanded. Lester picked a peel out of his bowl. "No food fights!"

Lillian woke up and began to cry. Comfort left Tyne's side, where she had been assisting in the crust crimping, and picked her daughter up. Rick frowned.

"Sorry," the two men said, their faces flushing slightly.

"Back to work, folks," Marge added, her hands spinning a roller across the pastry board. "How about *The Little Drummer Boy*?"

"Good idea," Estelle said. "It should be simple enough for chef Lester."

The choir started softly, building the rhythmic song gradually. Lillian soon fell asleep. Following Barb's direction, Paul and Uncle Miltie provided a counter beat, tapping out and humming the drum roll. As the main voices died out, the duo continued slowly, finishing their double-drum tattoo. Comfort began clapping and everyone cheered.

"Bravo!" Don and Lester cried. "Bravo!"

Grinning like fools, Paul and Uncle Miltie shook hands and took a little bow.

Gracie moved swiftly back and forth, checking and replenishing supplies, marking bags and generally keeping everyone's spirits up. She loved being busy and surrounded by dear friends—and it was most wonderful when they were all working together for a good cause.

"This is great," Marge said. "Isn't it?"

They continued making pies and singing carols for another hour and a half. Finally, the last pie was prepared, wrapped and labeled.

"I'm all pied out," Marge admitted, taking out a large coffeepot. "But I think I could stand a cookie—or maybe even two. How about you guys?"

"Swell gingersnaps, Gracie," Don said. "You were smart to bring a treat that bears very little resemblance to a pie!"

Cookie in hand, Uncle Miltie grinned. "Hey, you Turners. Which side of a pie is the right side?"

Tish and Tyne stared at him blankly.

"The one that gets eaten, because the other side is left!"

The twins turned their backs on him precisely at the same instant.

The door to the kitchen opened. Trent Freeman, his face shiny red from the cold, peeked in, obviously looking for Gracie.

"Hello there, Trent!" she said. "Please join us."

The boy hesitated, his glance swiftly taking in the others. "I don't mean to interrupt. I'm halfway finished, Pastor

Meyer, and I was just wondering if I could have some water?"

"Of course. Come in!" Paul stood to reach in the cupboard for a glass.

"Hungry?" Marge asked shrewdly.

"Of course he is," Marybeth replied. "Come. Sit down and have some of these ginger cookies."

"Well . . ." Trent still hesitated, then shucked his boots and coat and slipped onto an empty chair.

"Everyone," Gracie called out. "This is Trent Freeman, a whiz with a shovel."

Trent chewed silently.

"He's raising money to buy Christmas presents, aren't you, Trent? Having him has been a real blessing to me. He clears my walk every time it covers over again."

Trent nodded. "I'd be happy to help anyone else out."

"He charges reasonably," Marge added.

"Hello, Trent," Don said.

"Oh, hello, Mr. Delano," the boy replied.

"How are your sisters?"

Trent chewed. "Fine." He stared at the stacked pies. "What are you all doing here?"

"We're making pies to sell," Estelle explained.

He nodded. "You going to open up a bakery or something?"

Barb shook her head. "The money's going to charity."

Trent whistled under his breath. "You're spending

a Saturday making pies and then *giving* the money away?"

Paul cleared his throat. "Giving to others, especially those less fortunate, is very important. You know that."

"I guess," the boy said, considering the truth in what the minister had said but still looking doubtful.

Don offered, "I teach Bridget, you know." He added as an explanation for the others, "That's Trent's older sister. A really nice girl."

Trent reached for another gingersnap.

"I've seen you before," Lester said.

"You have?" Trent asked. "I don't think I've seen you."

"I'm sure! Give me a minute. I'll remember. It's on the tip of my tongue."

"So, you live with your aunt, young man?" Estelle asked.

"Uh huh. She's the best. Takes care of me and my sisters." He was watching Lester. "Most of the money I'm earning is going toward a gift for her."

Gracie, meanwhile, had had a thought and turned to Marybeth. "Has your mom found her bracelet yet?" she asked.

Marybeth shook her head. "It's still missing. What can I do? I keep pushing Herb to try to find it, but with the storms, there have been too many accidents and other problems to deal with." She sighed into her coffee mug. "Anyway, he's convinced she's mislaid it. I can't really blame him, you know? He found it for her once, but this time it seems really gone."

"Lost what?" Rick asked.

"My mom's bracelet. She lost it at the senior center. Again."

"Not the one with the lovely emerald?" Comfort asked, breaking off a cookie edge for the suddenly squirming Lillian.

"Yes, that one," Marybeth said glumly. "Everyone in town has been shown it sometime, somewhere."

"I've met your mom at the center," Comfort explained. "On kids' days."

"Oh, of course!" Marybeth replied.

"Lillian loves Mrs. Simmons. She sits on her lap and plays with all her jewelry."

Marybeth nodded. "My mom's crazy about babies."

"Speaking of babies," Estelle interrupted. "Who's playing the Christ Child this year?"

"I thought you knew," Paul said. "We're using a doll this year."

"Very wise," said Marybeth. Gracie nodded in agreement.

Barb rose and began piling dishes. "Everyone has their holiday robe?" All the choir members except Lester nodded. "Les? Where's yours?"

He frowned. "At home, I guess. I'm just not sure where. But I always find it in time, don't worry."

Gracie and Marge collected the last pieces of dirty cutlery and dishes. Paul and Rick began putting the dry dishes away.

"Ahem!"

The gang paused, looking in the direction of Uncle Miltie's voice.

Their elderly friend had laid a misshapen bag on the table by his coffee cup.

I'VE BEEN THINKING," Uncle Miltie said. "Those kids who participate in the pageant. Wouldn't it be nice to give them something to remember it by?"

"Sure," Paul answered. "What do you have in mind?"

Uncle Miltie reached into the netting and pulled out a small, winged statue, its hands clasped together in prayer. Trent Freeman leaned forward.

"Why, it's an *angel*!" Tish and Tyne cried simultaneously.

He handed one to each twin.

"They're identical," Tish exclaimed.

Tyne laughed. "Just like us."

Uncle Miltie smiled and passed a third angel to Gracie.

She turned the glistening white figure in her hands, recognizing the golden halo, brown hair and light-blue eyes. "But . . . but I thought they'd all been smashed?"

Her uncle's eyes twinkled. "So did I but . . . I'd forgotten that I had three still in the kiln. Flo found them. Do you think the kids would like them?"

"Like them?" Marge cried. "Why, Uncle Miltie, they're darling! Absolutely darling."

The rest approached and admired the statues. Trent asked if he could hold one. Tyne passed him one with a warning about its fragility. Trent examined it very closely.

"You made these yourself?" Comfort asked, holding another angel so Lillian could stroke its halo. "Careful, honey," she cautioned.

Uncle Miltie nodded proudly. "I've been taking pottery lessons. I had a bunch more, but some hooligan destroyed them."

"Oh, yes," Marybeth said. "Herb told me about it. Nasty business."

"It was," Gracie agreed. "Shocking."

Trent pushed his chair back. "I'd better go finish shoveling. Thanks."

Gracie jumped up and assisted him into his heavy quilted jacket. As she held it for him, an envelope fell from the pocket.

Trent grabbed for it.

"I'm sorry!" Gracie exclaimed, reaching down. "Let me help." Her fingers reached it before his did, and as the boy pulled it from her, Gracie blinked, uncertain of what she was seeing. The name 'Harriet Kimball' was written in a distinctive looping style across the envelope, over and over again, front and back.

Trent shoved the envelope back into his pocket. Mumbling goodbye, he hurried out.

Puzzled, Gracie walked back to the table, barely hearing the others. Her mind was focused on the signatures.

"I agree that these would be wonderful mementos," Paul was saying. "Do you think you can make enough before the pageant?"

The older man thought a moment. "Probably. If Gracie can spare me, I should have enough time. Mind if I leave them here, Paul?"

The pastor eyed the ceramic celestial trio. "Sure. I'd say they're right at home."

"Gracie?"

"Sorry?" Gracie replied, recalling her uncle's words with a bit of an effort. "Oh, of course I can spare you, dear."

"Any more dishes?" Barb wanted to know.

"He's working awfully hard," Rick said, watching Trent through the window.

"He's a good kid," Don replied. "But he and his sisters have had a pretty tough life, especially this past year."

"What happened?" Barb asked.

"Well, the father ran off when they were little. Never been heard from since. The littlest one had just been born."

Tish and Tyne sighed heavily, each whispering, "Poor baby."

"And that's just the start. Their mom died early last year and—"

"Oh, how awful!" Comfort cried. "Orphans!"

Don nodded. "Luckily, their aunt's been taking care of them." He glanced at Gracie who was stacking plates in the cupboard. "Have you met her?"

Gracie shook her head. "We haven't even spoken. I called the house, but she was out. Trent speaks very fondly of her, though."

Don paused, looking thoughtful. "Yeah. That's interesting."

"Why?" Marge asked, looking up from wiping off the tables.

"Well, when the aunt first arrived, I somehow got the impression that she was very strict. And I overheard one of Bridget's friends call her 'a neat freak.' Bridget rarely speaks of her, which isn't unusual, for a teenager, but . . ."

"But what?" This from Uncle Miltie.

Don removed his glasses, dipped them into the soapy water then rubbed them with a dry towel. "Lately, Bridget, too, can't say enough good things about her aunt."

"Isn't that a positive step?"

"I guess so, Marybeth. The turnabout's just a bit odd."

"Well, it's the odds that seem stacked against them," said Gracie. "But perhaps they're finally starting to make the proper emotional adjustments." She noticed the kitchen clock. "Dear me! I promised you all that we'd be finished by two and it's nearly quarter after." She gazed fondly at her friends. "I'd like to thank each and every one of you. I'm sure by our fund-raising efforts we will be able to enrich a local family's Christmas."

"Oh, Gracie, dear," the twins chimed, "we thank you for organizing our pie bee."

"A round of applause, my friends," Marge suggested. "For all of us."

Led by an excited Lillian, the pie-bee team clapped heartily.

They began to divide up the pies for storage. Barb and Marybeth put two dozen in the church's freezer. Then everyone packed a share for carrying home.

"Remember," Marge said, "no eating! Or no profits!"

In the parking lot, Gracie heard Don shouting for Trent, then Rick's baritone calling out that he was gone. After that, silence.

Gracie and Uncle Miltie were the last to leave. Flicking off the lights and balancing her pies, she plunged with her uncle into the frosty afternoon. As the crisp air caught her throat, a quote from the latest *Guideposts* popped into her head.

Friends are like angels without any wings. Blessing our lives with the most precious things. She repeated it out loud.

"They sure are!" she affirmed, opening the door to Fannie Mae. Her uncle, however, seemed lost in his own thoughts.

"THANK YOU," Pastor Paul said, as the choir's voices drifted into silence. "That was lovely." He looked down. His congregation waited expectantly. "Well, my friends. We're quickly moving into the Christmas season." He smiled at a gurgling baby in the front row. "It's a time of joy, of renewal, of sharing with our friends and families. For most of us, anyway."

He paused, his expression darkening. "But for many, it can be a time of broken promises, sadness and even depression—much of it caused by too-great expectations." He moved in front of his pulpit. "And these expectations themselves are fueled by slick advertising and merchandising targeted specifically to tug at our heartstrings, while making us loosen our purse strings! They grab us emotionally, but they also mock the pain many feel at this time of year. Now, I'm not saying crush those great expectations or muffle your hopes. Expectations should be great. What I'd like, though, is to encourage you to find your desires in the true spirit of Christmas, in the birth of our dear Lord, Himself. Express your Christmas spirit in simple acts of kindness, perhaps a small sacrifice or giving aid to another. Then, and only then, will your expectations be met beyond measure."

"Amen," an older woman whispered. Several others nodded.

"Now, in this spirit of giving, I want to remind you that, at Gracie Parks' initiative . . . "—several hands clapped—"our wonderful choir spent much of yesterday making a multitude of delicious pies. I was there so I can attest to the love that went into them. The frozen pies will be for sale following the Christmas pageant, and all money collected will go to a local needy family. So, please, come to the pageant and consider buying a pie. Your family will thank you—they'll wish you'd bought several!—and you'll help share in the meaning of Christmas." He glanced up at the choir loft.

Barb raised her baton. Everyone took a breath, and then the sopranos began singing the opening lines of *It Is So Sweet To Trust in Jesus*. Gracie and the Turner twins waited, then added their melodious altos, warming and harmonizing with the higher voices. Lester and Rick followed suit, their powerful tenors lending body and depth. Finally, Don and Bert Benton's potent baritones slid in underneath, supporting them all.

As they neared the end, the voices dropped off in reverse order until Amy Cantrell's soaring soprano was the only sound reverberating in the hushed sanctuary.

Finally, silence.

Then a sudden explosion of applause.

The choir members cheered.

"Excellent," Barb said after church, her eyes shining. "We should have a pie bee every week! Great way to practice."

"I don't know," Lester replied, flexing his fingers with a grimace. "Don't think I could tackle another pile of pastry."

The others laughed and began removing their robes.

"Hey, everyone!" Don called. "I need to know who's going to the county craft fair next Saturday. I want to organize the transportation."

"You don't have to worry about us," Tish said.

"We're not able to go," added Tyne.

"I'm in," Gracie called, pushing her sheet music into a folder. "And Uncle Miltie will want to come, too."

"Always," Don replied with a smile.

After some discussion, it was finally agreed that Gracie, her uncle, Marge, Barb, Estelle and Lester would all go together in Don's van.

"Wish I could," Amy sighed. "But I told Abe I'd do an extra shift at the deli."

"It sounds like a lot of fun," Bert said. "Too bad my brother's coming."

"Make sure whenever you go you drive carefully," Pastor Paul told them, as he mounted the steps into the loft. "I wouldn't want anything to happen to these heavenly voices. You were excellent, today, my friends. As usual."

"Gracie?" Paul asked. "May I speak with you for a minute?"

"Sure," she replied, waving to the others as they trooped down the stairs. "That was a lovely sermon, Paul. I liked how you brought our pies together with the true gift of Christmas."

"Thank you. Sometimes people don't like to be reminded of those less fortunate." He sighed, then straightened. "I was wondering if you'd be able to cater the Christmas pageant? I know you're going to be singing and all, but I think simple sandwiches and some desserts would be enough. I'll ask the others to help out with the eggnog and punch."

Gracie considered. "Okay, Paul. On one condition."

The young minister's face fell.

"Just don't ask for any more pie."

He laughed and squeezed her arm. "I'll leave the choices up to your superior judgment."

They began descending the stairs. "Tell me, did the Freemans attend the early service? I know Trent said they would try. I don't want to be a busybody, but I did ask him about whether or not they attended church. He was a little defensive—but hearing that they were fellow worshipers at Eternal Hope, at the early service, made me feel that maybe that aunt knew what she was doing, after all."

Paul shook his head. "Funny, after seeing him the other day, I realized that they actually haven't been here for quite a while." He looked pensive. "I really should have noticed and called Mrs. Kimball." He frowned. "I should listen to my own sermons."

"Don't be so hard on yourself, Paul. You've got a pretty large congregation. It's tough to keep track of every family. I didn't even know that family, myself."

"It's my job, isn't it? Keeping watch over my flock. Well, I'm going to take my own advice and give Mrs. Kimball a call." He stared out the main doors into the brilliant sunshine. "No time like the present. If you'll excuse me, Gracie." Paul shook Uncle Miltie's hand and strode swiftly back up the aisle.

"Paul!" Uncle Miltie called out. The pastor turned. "I thought your sermon was right on the mark!" Their minister smiled and disappeared into his office.

The parking lot was nearly empty. Gracie waved good-bye to Lester as he maneuvered his truck onto the street. "You're right," Gracie said, opening the door for her uncle and grabbing the snow brush. "But he realized he was preaching to himself and not just the congregation."

Later that afternoon, Gracie finished cutting an onion, washed her hands and then carefully dabbed her eyes. She was alone, having dropped her uncle at friends' on the way back from church. They would bring him home. A golden hue of light spilled through her kitchen window. Suddenly, Gooseberry arrived, streaking down the stairs and leaping onto his favorite seat to bask in the warm glow. Gracie stared out the window, past her front lawn and across the street, enchanted by the dazzling reflections twinkling off snow-gilded trees and dangling bluish icicles.

It was time to think about getting some dinner started. She slipped a pat of butter into a heated frying pan and added the onions to sauté. Then, after thinly slicing two large zucchini, she dumped them into the pan. Keeping the flame low, she let her mind wander as she stirred the vegetables. She kept seeing the scrawled-upon envelope that had fallen out of Trent Freeman's coat. It seemed fairly obvious that someone, in all likelihood Trent, was practicing his aunt's signature. But why?

She opened a can of corn. Perhaps he'd received a disappointing report card and didn't dare show her. Her own son, Arlen, had tried a similar trick many years ago but had been so overcome by guilt that he had confessed even before handing the forged report card in.

Adding some ground meat, Gracie pondered possible answers to the question of what Trent was up to. Maybe, she decided, it's simply none of my business. *I'm pretty sure, Lord, that You've put Trent on my doorstep for a reason. He's a troubled young man, and, as You know, I haven't dealt with someone his age in a long time. But I'm here to do Your bidding. If there's anything specific You want me to do, please let me know. In the interim, I'll continue along, following what I hope is Your path.*

And a well-shoveled one at that, she thought mischievously.

As her meal simmered, thickened with a can of plum tomatoes, she focused her thoughts on food for the upcoming pageant, especially the desserts. Given the number and ages of the attendees, simple, easy-to-handle treats were best. Festive cinnamon stars, iced-cookie trees and chocolate-cherry fudge squares were easy, but what else? Something truly special. Her mind raced through the possibilities. Christmas cake? Maybe, though it wasn't as popular as it used to be. Something colorful for the youngsters? She glanced outside at the icicles dripping in the sun. She had it! Drop mints, especially if they were dyed in Christmas colors.

As she considered the Nativity pageant, she drained off the extra liquid and then turned the heat low under the pan. Eternal Hope's pageant offered its audience a boxlike stall padded with straw, the various children dressed up and playing their specific roles, and the choir singing in the background. The animals, however, were pretty old and tattered: a couple of balding plush toy lambs and a rickety extra-large Eeyore acting the part of the donkey. Remembering Rocky's comment, she chuckled, visualizing his stocky figure on all fours and draped in a gray blanket.

Then she remembered some oversized molds she'd seen in

Uncle Miltie's pottery class. Some were animals. Perhaps Flo could make something ceramic, maybe a few lambs or a camel or two? Would they be large enough, though?

She carefully drained some of the liquid from the pan into the sink. Wiping her hands, she picked up the phone.

Florence Jackson answered on the first ring.

Before Gracie barely had gotten out a hello, she was interrupted.

"Oh," Flo told her, "a lovely thing has happened."

"What's happened?"

"I've just this very minute had a visitor. Mr. Gravino from the *Mason County Gazette* came over because he wants to write an article on me. Seems the paper's doing a series on local artists. Someone—he wouldn't say who but I think I can guess—gave him my name."

Gracie realized that Flo believed Uncle Miltie had suggested her name to Rocky. She didn't know whether she should tell the truth or let her uncle take the credit. She decided that Uncle Miltie deserved a little admiration. "Congratulations! I can't wait to read it."

"I'm not sure when it'll be published, but I'll let you know. Oh, dear, I'm so sorry, Gracie. I've been rattling on. And *you* called *me*."

"Yes," Gracie replied. She heard the front door open and close. Her uncle's deep voice called out a greeting. "And I'm glad I did. It was wonderful to hear your good news." She paused, uncertain if now was a good time to ask Florence for help.

"Well?"

Uncle Miltie arrived in the kitchen and headed to the stove. He looked under the lid and inhaled. Gracie signaled for him to take a wooden spoon and stir the cooked ingredients. "I don't want you to think I'm taking advantage but . . . I was wondering if you might consider helping out Uncle Miltie and me? Our church, really."

"After what he's done for me," Flo answered, "I'd be glad to lend a hand. What can I do?"

"Well, Eternal Hope holds a Christmas pageant every year and, though the spirit of the season's there in full, I must admit parts of our Nativity scene are where we are a bit threadbare."

"*Umm.*"

The enthusiasm in Flo's voice had faded. Gracie feared it was due to the mention of church. "You don't have to attend or anything," she added quickly. "Though of course, we'd be delighted to welcome you. But what I really need are some new animals for the manger."

"Animals?"

"You know . . . lambs, a cow or two, possibly a camel, if that's not pushing it."

There was a pause then Flo laughed softly. "Oh! I get it.

You need some clay figures for your Nativity scene, right? Sure. I'd be delighted."

"Bless you," Gracie replied gratefully. "As large as you can mold them would be wonderful, but we can put them in the back, as though they were some distance away. I'll let you decide on what and how many, okay? How about we touch base sometime next week? Thanks again! And good luck with the interview."

She hung up.

"This looks mighty good," Uncle Miltie said.

"There's going to be some hot bread, too."

His eyes shone, and he rubbed his hands. "Dee-licious. But who was that?"

"Flo. She's agreed to make some animals for the manger."

"Great. Once I've got my angels made, I'll give her a hand." He started setting the table. "*What* interview? Isn't that what you said?"

Gracie paused and decided honesty was the best policy. As always. "Rocky's going to write a column about her, as part of a new series on local artists I suggested."

"Wonderful! I think you did mention it, but I didn't know he had taken you up on it. I'll have to give him a call."

Gracie nodded, but she looked uneasy.

He hesitated, a fork remaining in his right hand. "I get the feeling I'm missing something."

Gracie sighed. "Flo thinks it was *your* idea to do it."

His eyes widened. "I should set her straight."

Gracie shook her head.

"I'd rather you get the credit," she assured him. "You're already my hero, and now you can be hers, too."

GINGERBREAD MEN ARE A MUST," Marge Lawrence said. It was late morning and Marge was leaning back in one of Gracie's kitchen chairs, nursing her second cup of coffee. Two sheets of paper—one marked *Gracie*, the other *Marge*—and a pen were at her side.

"Of course!" Gracie said, sitting across from her. "How did I forget them? Probably because I always start fading after the first batch."

Her friend smiled and twirled the shiny bracelets lining her left arm. "You leave them to me."

Uncle Miltie moved the newspaper, which had been covering his face, and gave his niece a broad wink.

"All right. So we're agreed that you're going to make, *hmm*, let's say three dozen?" Her friend nodded, sipping for a moment. "Might as well make the cinnamon-sugar cookies, too. I've got the star cookie cutters in a couple of sizes." Marge scrawled a few words on her piece of paper. "How about two dozen each?"

"You're a dear, thanks. I'll handle the trees and the fudge, say two pounds? And the drop mints. More coffee, anyone?" Gracie asked, filling up her own cup.

"Gracie," Marge said, changing the subject. "I'm not sure what's up with that boy, Trent. Have you noticed that he's always starving? I end up feeding him every time he finishes my walk. It's as though he hasn't had a decent meal in a week."

"Practically eats us out of house and home, too, isn't that right, Gracie?" Uncle Miltie chimed in.

His niece nodded. "He does eat a lot, but I just put it down to his age. Arlen ate like a horse when he was thirteen."

"And he wears the same old sweat shirt and worn-out jeans day after day."

Uncle Miltie chuckled. "I wouldn't worry about that, Marge. Probably some new fad. He's a good kid. It's more than I can say for some of them around here."

"It *is* odd," Gracie said. "Especially after what Don said about Trent's aunt being a 'neat freak.' There's something not quite right, I agree—even if I don't have much experience with today's teens."

She hesitated, thinking. "Sometimes Trent will start to say something—it seems like it could be important—and then he clams up. At other times, he'll ask the most bizarre questions."

"Like what?" Marge asked, leaning forward.

"Well, the other day, he asked me the cost of two yards of purple satin but wouldn't explain why. Of course, I didn't know offhand, but I inquired and when I called him to let him know, I got the answering machine, as usual." She sighed.

"The same thing happened to me. Trent forgot his wool cap the other day and when I phoned to let him know, I had to leave a message. By the way, have you ever spoken to his aunt? The way he goes on and on about her, she must be something pretty special."

Gracie shook her head. "What she does is a mystery to me, since she doesn't even have the courtesy to reply to the phone calls." The others looked at her expectantly. Gracie shrugged. "I guess it's really just a little thing but . . . I left her one about contributing to the pie-bee supplies. I never heard back from her."

"It doesn't make much sense, does it?" Marge wondered aloud. "If she's such a paragon, you'd think she'd at least return a telephone call. Especially from someone who's befriended her nephew."

"You two are jumping to conclusions, *as usual*," Uncle Miltie declared. "The poor woman's obviously run off her feet. Stepping in to raise three kids after their mother has died. No wonder, she forgot your message. Besides," he added, snapping open the paper. "You don't even know if she got it, do you? One of the kids probably forget to tell her. It could be as simple as that."

Although Gracie nodded her agreement, she couldn't help believing in her heart that there was more to it.

Much more.

ALTHOUGH GRACIE WAS DRESSED for the icy weather and had kept a brisk pace during her after-lunch walk, she was relieved to see the partially frosted window of Abe's Deli as she rounded the last corner. Eyes tearing from the wind, she blinked through half-frozen eyelashes and recognized the small black sedan belonging to Rocky Gravino parked directly outside. Her spirits rose even further.

Pulling the handle, she was greeted by a desperate gasp from the inhabitants inside. "Shut the door!" a voice shouted.

"Quick!" another shrieked.

Gracie did so, then stood for a moment, adjusting to the light and shaking out her curls. Her fingers and cheeks tingled. The smells were delightful. She would soon be human again, but how would she make herself walk outside again?

"Gracie!" Abe Wasserman called. "Come in. Come in!" Her friend stepped quickly around the counter and gently helped remove her coat. "You've been walking," he said, his tone accusatory. "It's too cold for that nonsense. Over here. I'll get you a nice bowl of hot barley soup to start, okay?"

She was about to object, but he escorted her to a back booth where Rocky was deep in conversation with Herb Bower. Two plates with half-eaten sandwiches and a few ketchup-laden french fries rested between them.

The two men looked up, then clambered to their feet. Gracie shooed them back down.

"Gracie!" Rocky said, face brightening. "Good grief! You look like a woman-shaped icicle! Sit down."

Gracie glanced at Herb. "I don't want to int—"

"Your timing couldn't be better, Gracie," Herb said, making room on his side of the booth.

"Bless you," she told Abe, reaching to take a steaming bowl from him. She almost dropped it from the shock of the heat.

She looked expectantly at Herb first, then Rocky.

Herb turned to her. "You know the back window of your church?"

She had slipped through that very window on more than one occasion when locked out. Surely, the police chief didn't know? Gracie sipped cautiously and nodded, glad that she hadn't refused the soup. It was delicious, as usual. Bless Abe.

"Want part of my sandwich?" Rocky asked, pushing his plate in her direction.

She shook her head.

"After the last break-in, my recollection is that a lock was supposed to be put on that window." Herb was finishing a grilled cheese on rye.

"I believe Paul said something about it, yes." More soup slid into her stomach, warming her entire body.

Abe reappeared. "What else? A piece of poppyseed cake?"

"Oh, no thanks, Abe. I already had lunch. The soup's perfect, thanks. It's a magic elixir. Going to join us?"

"Love to—" A pair of customers approached his register. "In a minute," he said, hurrying off.

"Why'd you ask about the window?"

"Somebody made use of it again for entry into the church. It could have been avoided if that lock had been installed as recommended."

Gracie gasped. "Oh dear! Was there much damage?"

Herb seemed startled. "Funny you should ask. Most people immediately tend to think what's missing."

Gracie shrugged. "There's not much to steal." She looked at both men. "So, what happened?"

"Well, Pat Allen dropped by to pick something up and

found the kitchen floor covered in pieces of pottery. She didn't know what they were."

"Pieces of pottery?" Gracie asked, her mind whirling.

"Uh huh. Smashed to bits." Herb shook his head. "I've told Marybeth many times. The church really should tighten up its security."

It was Gracie's turn to be startled. She set her soup spoon down with a decisive clang. "God's house is for everyone, Herb Bower! Especially the desperate. You know that. It's bad enough that Paul feels the need to take some church property home for safekeeping and that the front doors are locked most of the time! But to shut our Lord's house up tighter than Fort Knox." She shook her red curls. "No. That's not right."

Rocky threw Herb a cautionary look.

The police chief hesitated, then sighed. He knew Gracie too well.

Gracie calmed down, her curiosity overcoming her exasperation. "Do you know *what* was broken?" she asked. She might guess, but, still, it seemed too fantastical.

"I asked Paul, but he didn't recognize anything." Herb reached into his pocket and pulled out a partially rounded white shard.

"May I?" she asked, reaching.

"Be my guest," Herb replied, dropping it into her outstretched palm.

Gracie carefully fingered the bit.

"You know what it is." Rocky said. "I can see it in your face."

"Well?" Herb asked.

"Remember the incident at the senior center? The bits and pieces scattered on the floor?"

Herb nodded. "Some figurines were broken, right? Sounded like a practical joker to me. I must admit, I didn't pay serious attention. You think this is related?"

Although she knew part of the answer, Gracie remained silent, trying to figure it all out. After thirty seconds, she let out a deep breath. It was like attempting to put the broken pieces of ceramic back together!

"Come on, Gracie," Rocky prompted. "Give."

"Well, it's only a suggestion. Uncle Miltie has a new hobby," she began to explain. "Pottery. Florence Jackson's the name of his teacher. He's been making things . . . pots, platters. Most recently, *angels*."

Herb watched her expectantly.

"You don't seem to remember, Herb, but it was Uncle Miltie's angels that were broken at the senior center."

"Angels? Oh, yeah. Right."

"So?" Rocky asked, waving his empty coffee mug at Abe, who was holding up the pot.

"So, three of his angels were safe and sound in the kiln.

Uncle Miltie hadn't realized that right away. He brought them to show us at the pie-making bee."

"Marybeth has her eyes on some of those pecan pies," Herb said. "Myself, even though it's past Thanksgiving, I always favor the pumpkin."

"Forget the pies," Rocky said. "What about the angels?"

"Uncle Miltie left them at the church." She frowned. "He thought they were safe there."

"So, let me get this straight," the police chief said, barely containing a grin. "Your uncle's angels are at the center of this? Do they tell bad jokes, too?"

Gracie made as if to swat him on the arm.

"Hey!" Herb said, pulling back with mock pain. "Striking a peace officer's against the law."

"You deserved it," Rocky replied. "Let's back up a minute, Gracie. You said Flo Jackson's teaching Uncle Miltie?"

She nodded.

"Great! Think he'd mind speaking to me about her? Some anecdotes from a student would add texture to my story."

"You'd better bring an extra pad of paper," Gracie replied. "He *loves* her. He'll probably talk your ear off. I'm on my way over to the center, if you want to come."

"I'll give you a lift."

Herb's cell phone beeped. "Well, better get going. Not sure what to say about the angels being targeted, Gracie. I still think it's some punk, but I'd encourage you to ask Pastor Paul to rethink that lock. There's not much we can do if the church doesn't take the proper precautions."

He got up, paid his bill and left, trailed by a protest of voices as more cold air raced inside.

13

AS THE NEWSPAPER OWNER expertly drove the icy streets, Gracie leaned back, relishing the role of passenger. The black sedan was small, so Rocky's broad shoulders almost touched hers, creating a familiar companionship she appreciated. Their friendship was important to her.

Though just shy of his seventh decade, Rocky's thick, longish hair was only partially grey, his eyes clear, hands steady. She hadn't felt this comfortable with a man, other than her uncle, in many years. If only he shared her love and interest in God, as her adored Elmo had.

"Warm enough?"

She nodded. "How's the article on Flo going, anyway? I happened to speak to her just after you called. She was absolutely thrilled."

"I'm the one who's thrilled," he replied. "She gave a great

interview. Very articulate, good sense of humor . . . but it's the way she speaks about her art!" He paused. "I have to admit, Gracie. I'm more of a paint-by-numbers sort of fellow. But to see such passion for an artistic endeavor here in Willow Bend. . . ."

"I know," Gracie replied. "And it's contagious. Uncle Miltie's caught a dose of it, at least."

"I . . . I've interviewed a lot of folks—politicians, athletes, average citizens, even a few artists. I don't think until now that I've ever really understood before. You know what Pablo Picasso said?"

Gracie shook her head.

"He said that every child's an artist, but that the problem is how to remain an artist once you've grown up. I think I finally understand, thanks to Florence Jackson."

Gracie thought of her uncle and of how he had raved about his teacher. Now, she realized, the eighty-year-old might even be carrying a torch. Flo Jackson *was* a striking woman. And how vulnerable as a widow she might seem, especially to older men. There was no reason Rocky should be exempt. Alone for some years, he himself was vulnerable.

"Did you know," Rocky asked, "that she's a fly-fishing expert?" He laughed heartily. "Doesn't that beat all? Imagine, those slender fingers tying a Green-sedge Goodie!"

"No," Gracie replied coolly. "I can't imagine. My mind's too occupied with trying to understand who would deliberately seek out and smash my uncle's ceramic pieces."

He considered this. "You don't agree with Herb's theory."

"Why just the angels?" Gracie shook her head. "No, I'm afraid there's something more serious at work than Herb's punk."

Rocky stopped the car. "Like what?" They had arrived at the senior center.

"I don't know, but it could be someone harboring anti-Christian sentiments, trying to send a message."

Rocky almost smiled. "If I were going to make some sort of anti-Christian statement, I don't think I'd target an elderly fellow's pottery. Besides, if I were later going to break into a church, I'd do a lot more damage to the sanctuary and altar, don't you think?"

Gracie stared through the windshield. Finally, she nodded. "I see your point. But who else knew about the angels in the church, other than the participants in the pie bee?"

Rocky shrugged. "You don't suspect any of them, do you?"

"Of course not." She paused. "I guess it's possible that someone from the center is upset with Uncle Miltie."

This time Rocky didn't resist the urge to smile. "That's more like it! I've seen your uncle play pinochle."

"I'm serious!"

"Okay! Okay! Just kidding!" He patted her arm. "I know

you are, Gracie. It's just I think you're getting yourself far too worked up over a childish prank."

Gracie didn't see any point in further discussion. "Come on," she said, pushing open the door. "It's suddenly very cold in here."

"Bridget!" Gracie exclaimed, recognizing the young woman polishing the floor near the entrance.

Bridget Freeman looked up and smiled shyly. She glanced quickly around, then shut off the machine

"It's Mrs. Parks," Gracie said, extending her hand. "Trent's been clearing my sidewalk. Remember?" She paused, mouth widening. Dark smudges underlined the teenager's eyes. Her hair looked stringy, her sweater stained.

"Oh, yes. Hello, Mrs. uh ... Parks."

"Bridget, dear, I'd like you to meet Rocky Gravino."

Rocky shook her hand. "My pleasure, young lady."

"Mr. Gravino's editor of the *Gazette*."

"Oh?" Bridget replied blankly.

"The newspaper. He's the owner and editor. He's been working on an article on Mrs. Jackson."

Bridget's jaw dropped. "The newspa ... oh ..." She looked down.

"Any word on Mrs. Simmons's bracelet?" Rocky asked.

Bridget stiffened. The machine roared to life. "Sorry!" she

shouted, sliding the buffer from side to side. "I have to get back to work!"

"She seems a little frazzled for a teenaged girl. Do you think they work her too hard in here?" Rocky watched her for a minute.

"She's had a hard time, poor thing," Gracie replied, leading the way to the kiln room. "She has no parents, and she and her brother and sister are being raised by an aunt." She looked thoughtful. "It can't be easy."

"No," Rocky said, gently taking her arm. "I'm sure it isn't."

Gracie felt her cheeks flush and chided herself for her earlier, jealous thoughts.

"Rocky!" They heard Uncle Miltie's voice. "Come on in."

They stepped into the room to find Uncle Miltie and Florence Jackson hard at work testing glazes for a foot-high camel. Not just any old camel from a mold but a hand-sculpted, single-humped masterpiece. Gracie held her breath. She wouldn't have been surprised if the beast bent down to eat. "Notice the texture," Flo was saying, running her fingers along its curving neck. "And how the fire marks add to the overall beauty."

Gracie smiled at her uncle's intense and enthusiastic expression. Paintbrush in one hand, another between his teeth, his whole countenance throbbed with life. She decided to wait to tell him about the latest disaster to befall his angels. It was too precious a moment, as he displayed his artistic concentration and delight in new skills.

Running paint-stained fingers through her hair, Flo glanced up with a slight smile. Upon seeing Rocky, she beamed.

"Mr. Gravino!" She walked around the table and started to offer her hand. "How nice to see you," she added, hesitating as she noticed the amount of brown staining her palm.

He laughed and held up his own hands. "Call me Rocky, remember?"

"You've come for a tour?"

He nodded. "If that's convenient."

"For you, *any* time's convenient. Please, follow me."

Gracie approached her uncle. "That camel's amazing!"

He nodded, then took the paintbrush from his mouth. "Flo made it." He reached to a shelf below and pulled up a chubby lamb statue and then its twin. They were identical, glazed white with shiny black eyes and hooves, obviously crafted from a mold. "These are mine." He blew air out of his lips. "I have a hard enough time with my old fingers. But this," he stroked the camel lightly. "*This* is art."

"They're all lovely," Gracie said, touching a lamb. "The kids are going to adore them."

Flo was gesturing in the direction of Uncle Miltie. "Of course, none of this would be possible without my handsome assistant," she gravely informed Rocky.

Gracie's uncle blushed.

Flo gave him a quick squeeze across the shoulders. "He's been with the class from the beginning, always offering to help."

Gracie bit her lip.

"I'm hoping he'll agree to speak to me. For the article." Rocky turned to the elderly man. "What do you say, Uncle Miltie? Care to offer a few words about what working with Flo's meant to you? I think you're her favorite pupil."

Uncle Miltie looked proud.

His niece jumped in. "I told Rocky you'd be keen to be interviewed. Right, Uncle Miltie?"

"Keen? Why, Gracie, my dear, that doesn't come *close* to describing my feeling right now."

Now it was Florence Jackson's turn to blush.

HELLO, GRACIE," Pastor Paul's greeting came out of the answering machine. Gracie and Uncle Miltie had arrived home a few minutes earlier and now were slumped in kitchen chairs, exhausted. "Hello, Uncle Miltie. Hope you and the beautiful potter are both well," the voice added.

Uncle Miltie looked indignant.

The message continued. "Just kidding, Uncle Miltie. Look, I finally got around to checking out Mrs. Kimball's—the Freemans' aunt—work address and you know what? When I called, they told me that she was on extended leave. She's been away about a month."

Gracie and her uncle exchanged a surprised glance.

"I thought it was a little odd," Paul's message continued. "But they wouldn't give me any more information. Have you any idea where she might be? I've been hoping she'd return my calls but, so far, no success."

He hesitated. "No hurry. And thanks. See you both on Sunday." Click.

"Well, that's pretty bizarre," Gracie said, her brow furrowed. "Don't you think?

Her uncle nodded his agreement.

Gracie nodded. "On several occasions, both Trent and Bridget have mentioned that their aunt was at work. And that's been in the past month."

Gooseberry leapt into her lap, curled into position and promptly fell asleep. Gracie stroked him automatically, unhappy as a jarring thought kept bothering her.

"Something's going on. Those kids are lying to us. Why?" She looked at her uncle, and he recognized a familiar stubborn expression that meant she intended to find out.

Uncle Miltie grunted. "I think you're overreacting. Kids tell tales all the time. It doesn't necessarily mean anything. You know that." He stood and headed for the kettle. "Tea?"

Distracted, Gracie barely nodded.

"There could be half a dozen, no, a *dozen* reasons, why they aren't telling the truth. Teenagers really are like another species. Who knows what they're thinking?"

He shuddered as he reached for the ironstone sugar bowl. "Have you heard that horrible noise they call music? It's awful. It's not even *music*. Just someone shouting. And more often than not, it seems to promote violence."

"The Freeman kids aren't violent. And that's not what we're talking about."

"No." He popped two teabags into the pot, then carried the cookie jar to the table. "Of course not, but they *are* teenagers who probably find it easier to tell a lie than bother about the details of truth. Besides," Uncle Miltie continued, waiting for the water to boil, "it's none of our business."

Gracie's fingers tapped along Gooseberry's back.

"What are you thinking?"

"Just remembering something that was bothering me. When I spoke to the little girl, Trixie, my impression was that no one was home. I just wasn't properly reacting."

"So?" her uncle asked, pouring boiling water into the teapot. "What does that mean?"

Gracie gently removed the cat and plunked him onto a nearby chair. Pulling open the fridge door, she removed the milk. "Well, who was baby-sitting her, then? She's only eight. She can't be left alone." She laid the bottle on the table. "Do you mind pouring the tea while I give Paul a call?"

Her uncle nodded.

In a minute, Gracie heard the young pastor's voice. "Yes, hello, Paul. Just following up on your call about Mrs. Kimball. Her leave of absence is news to us. In fact, both kids have mentioned her being at work."

"That's odd."

"That's what Uncle Miltie and I've just been saying."

"Seems we're having our share of strange happenings, aren't we? What with the break-in and smashing of the angels and all."

"Do you have any idea yet who did it?"

"No. The police have once again encouraged me to have that window security-locked." He paused, breath coming out in a sigh. "Most parishioners choose the doors, anyway."

Gracie took a swallow of tea. "Those are nearly the exact same sentiments I expressed to Herb Bower not three hours ago."

"It's a shame, though, about the angels."

"Yes. I can't imagine why someone would go to all that trouble to break in just to destroy Uncle Miltie's angels—oh dear!" she exclaimed, suddenly aware of her uncle's astonished stare. "I . . . I've got to go, Paul. I'll let you know if I hear anything about Mrs. Kimball." She hung up before he could reply and turned to face her relative.

"What's that about? Did I hear you correctly?"

"I'm really sorry, I meant to tell you earlier at the center, but you were so happy . . . " She took a deep breath. "Someone got into the church and smashed your lovely little angels."

Uncle Miltie's face fell. "But they were the last ones."

She patted his arm. "I *am* sorry."

"This is getting ridiculous!" he fumed, slamming down his tea, splashing the table. "It's got to be somebody with a grudge. Nothing else makes sense." His eyes narrowed. "I bet you a plugged nickel it's either Mac Medline or Harry Mayhew."

"Mac? Harry?" Gracie asked, wiping the table clean. "Why in the world do you think it could be either of them?"

"Sore losers. Both of 'em."

She suddenly understood. "You don't think one of them's so upset over losing a pinochle game that he'd deliberately seek out and destroy your angels!"

He nodded, hands clenched into fists.

"Crawl through the back window of the church? Mac or Harry?!" Gracie couldn't contain her laughter at the image of either elderly man attempting to squeeze through the window frame. She gave him a hug. "Why don't we face facts? Neither of us has a clue."

"What? So we just wait until the good Lord reveals all?"

"I didn't say that," Gracie replied. "You know the Lord helps those who help themselves." She extended her arm. "The investigation into the mystery of the broken angels continues apace . . . is all I can say."

"Amen," he replied, vigorously shaking her hand.

NOOOELLL, NOOOELLLL, *born is the Kiiing of Isssraell."*

The voices stopped, but the beautiful harmonies continued to float through the van.

Goose pimples rippled along Gracie's arms. She shivered, not from the bitter cold outside the automobile, but from the pure joy inside, created by voices united in Christmas anthems.

It was late Saturday afternoon and her friends were returning from the craft fair in Mason City. More snow had started to fall in the past half hour, and now a cross wind had picked up, snatching and twisting the flakes and forming knee-high drifts along the road.

Gracie was thankful to be safely inside in the warm van. Outside as the daylight faded, she felt as though they were traveling through a desert of bluish-white sand, the stark, black silhouettes of the telephone poles and bare trees the only relief in an otherwise monochromatic landscape. Every few miles, a puff of chimney smoke hovered momentarily in the air before being torn to shreds by the winds.

At the wheel, Don drove cautiously, keeping well under the speed limit. The high school science teacher's face remained calm, but Gracie noticed that his gloves tightly gripped the steering wheel. She wondered if their carol singing was too much of a distraction.

"That was fantastic!" Barb cried. Though the choir director was sitting beside her on the middle seat, Gracie could barely make out her face. She shifted under the seat belt, her feet pressing against a pile of plastic bags filled with purchases. A car heading in the opposite direction passed then, its headlights temporarily blinding. The van shuddered, buffeted by both the other car and by the increasing winds.

"It must be something about the van's acoustics," Lester shouted from the front passenger seat. "It sounds just like a cathedral in here."

"How much—uh, uh, aah-chooo!—farther?" Marge asked, blowing her nose.

"God bless you!" the others chorused.

"In these conditions? Tough to say," Don replied, his eyes on the wind-stripped highway ahead.

"Anybody want another graham cracker?" Estelle asked from the back, handing the box to Gracie.

Sitting beside her, Uncle Miltie dug in. "Don't mind if I do. Thanks."

Gracie offered the box to Marge, who refused, then handed it to Lester. He extracted a broken piece which he handed to Don.

"What are you doing? Rationing?" Don laughed and popped it in his mouth.

Uncle Miltie prodded Gracie on the shoulder. "Did you see that booth with all the ceramics?"

She nodded. "Really liked the bowls, especially the one with the red streaks."

"Me, too." He paused and bit into his graham cracker. "They were pretty good, weren't they?"

"Well," Gracie replied, catching the anxiety in his voice, "yes, but nothing like Flo's work."

"No. Of course not but . . ." His voice faded into the dark.

"But what?" Marge asked, twisting her neck to see him.

"Oh . . . nothing," he replied.

Though she couldn't see his expression, Gracie recognized that tone of disappointment. She thought about it for a minute, then reassured him. "Your class's work is just as good," she said, silently asking for forgiveness for the little white lie.

Marge pointed out, "From what I hear, everything you've made has turned up broken. It's unfortunate . . . and very weird, I know, but true."

Miltie looked downcast. Gracie decided, as she often did, that Marge was a bit lacking in the diplomacy department.

"Any chance you could turn up the heat, Don?" Estelle shouted. "Don't know about Uncle Miltie, but I can't feel my feet."

"Don't worry about me," the elderly man replied. "My feelings are so crushed that not even this freezing weather could bother them."

"Oh, Uncle Miltie," Marge realized what she'd done. "I'm sorry. I didn't mean to upset you. Honest."

"Anybody seen my cell phone?" Lester asked, running his hands through his pockets and digging about the floor in front of him.

"I'm not sure. What's it look like?" Estelle asked sweetly.

"*Very* funny."

The others sang out "No!"

"Gee," Lester said, "could I have left it back there? I know I took it out when I needed something from that pocket. Did I put it down?"

Gracie saw headlights appearing ahead in the dark. The wind howled outside and snow swirls gusted, enveloping the car in white.

No one had seen what Lester had done with his phone.

"Heat's on full blast," Don shouted. "But I'll try and fiddle with one of these knobs. There must be a way to get more out of it!"

"Look out!" Lester yelled.

A horn blasted. Suddenly, the approaching headlights blazed dead ahead.

Don yanked the wheel to the right. A semitrailer thundered by, well across the center line. For a second, everyone was frozen in its high beams. The huge truck missed them by inches, then careened away.

The van spun out of control, and lurched violently off the road.

Estelle screamed.

With a sickening *bang*, the van hit a snowbank, turned ninety degrees, then ricocheted off another block of icy snow.

The front wheels came to a sliding halt as the damaged vehicle coughed, then died. They were facing the wrong way.

Someone moaned.

Outside, the wind snarled.

Then, silence buried them.

THE SILENCE WAS BROKEN by their panicked jumble of voices.

"Is everyone all right?" Don shouted, his voice thick with fear. "Gracie? Marge? Les? Bar—"

"My ankle!" Les answered. "Oww! I can't move it."

Don unhooked his seat belt, then lunged across to his friend. "You're caught. Just a sec—" He reached under the seat and gently dislodged Lester's foot.

Lester moaned.

"Sorry!" Don said, his head popping back up. "Better?"

Lester shifted, his face pale in the moonlight. "Yeah," he whispered, voice coming in a rush. "He didn't stop! Can you believe it? He practically ran us over and didn't even stop. What kind of a person does that?"

"Uncle Miltie!" Gracie was shouting, twisting in her seat. What she saw gave her a shock almost as severe as the impact of the van's unnatural halt. Estelle was sagging in her seat belt, one palm on her forehead. Blood streamed down her face. She groaned softly. Uncle Miltie's thick hands were clasped to his chest, his eyes wide with pain. A stab of panic ripped her heart. She feared he was having trouble breathing.

"Don, quick!" Gracie cried, tearing at her seat belt. "Estelle's bleeding! And Uncle Miltie's hurt, too!"

Marge had already freed herself and was scrambling over the seat, hankerchief in hand. In a couple of seconds, she had wedged herself into position and pressed the cloth against the gash in Estelle's head. Then she seized Gracie's jacket and pulled her up. Gracie reached over the seat and grabbed her uncle's hand.

"Uncle Miltie! Oh dear heaven, are you all right?"

"Help! I'm stuck."

Gracie realized the voice was Barb's.

"I'm okay," her uncle's voice replied weakly. "Just a sore chest. I must have hit the seat. Or maybe it hit me."

"My seat belt's jammed," the choir director said, her voice remarkably calm. "I can't move."

Don opened his door. Everyone gasped at the rush of bitterly cold air. "Hang on. I'm coming around."

Gracie reached down, fumbling for Barb's hand. She found

it and squeezed tightly. "Our Father," she whispered. "Who art in heaven, hallowed be Thy name."

"Thy Kingdom come. Thy will be done," Barb continued.

"On earth as it is in heaven," Marge added.

The others joined in and they finished the Lord's Prayer as one.

"Amen," Uncle Miltie gasped, struggling to stay calm.

Something outside rattled. Don's face appeared in the side window. There was another rattle and the van shifted slightly. He made a face and jabbed a gloved finger toward Lester and Barb. "Doesn't look too good!" he shouted, the wind snatching his words. He shook his head and disappeared.

A moment later, he climbed back into the driver's seat. He turned the ignition key. The engine clicked. Lester leaned forward. Don tried again. Nothing.

"Maybe it's flooded? Try holding down the accelerator," suggested Lester, gulping for breath.

Don did so. Gracie crossed her fingers. The engine sputtered, then died. Don tried again. And again. To no avail. Finally, he banged the steering wheel in frustration. "It's dead," he said dejectedly. "Marge? Gracie? How's it going back there?"

"Okay," Gracie replied, her fingers still clutching those of Barb and her uncle.

"Gracie, your cell phone!" Marge exclaimed.

"Oh!" Gracie replied, letting loose her grip on Barb's hand. She fumbled on the floor for her purse, yanking up bag after bag of presents and treats. Finally, she found it and dragged out the phone. She realized with an icy dread that she had forgotten to charge it. Would it work? All eyes stared as her shaking fingers hit the power button. The little red light didn't come on. "No!" she cried, punching the button again.

"What's wrong?" Estelle asked.

Gracie dialled 9-1-1 and held the receiver to her ear. She heard nothing, no dial tone, no voice. "Oh, I don't believe it . . . it's dead," she whispered, shaking the phone violently. Marge sighed.

"Wait," Les shouted. "I've got min—oh, no!" His tenor voice tumbled. "I left it at the craft fair, remember?"

"Oh, for heaven's sake! This is ridiculous!" Barb snapped, her eyes boring into Gracie's. "What's the point of having a cell phone if you're not going to properly care f—"

"All right. All right," Don interrupted. "There's no point blaming anyone. The way I see it, we've got to get help."

"Look!" Marge called out.

Everyone twisted in their seat to follow her outstretched hand. In the distance, the outline of a house could be seen in the twilight.

"It's a farm!" she shouted. "We're saved."

"Right!" Don said. "This is what we're going to do. Gracie,

you and I are going for help. Marge and Barb—you two stay and take care of the others. Okay?"

Gracie shuddered at the thought of stepping into the howling winds, but she buttoned up her heavy coat and wound her scarf tightly around her neck. Marge offered her a pair of sheepskin gloves she had just purchased for a friend.

"She won't mind," she said, giving Gracie a quick squeeze.

Gracie turned to her uncle. "You sure you're okay?"

He reassured her, "I'm fine. You be careful."

She threw him a kiss and turned to the door.

"Wait," Barb commanded.

Gracie spun around, trying not to wince at the sharp pain that suddenly stabbed her neck.

"Wear this," Barb said, taking off her wooly hat with adjustable ear flaps. "It should help against the wind." She hugged Gracie. "I'm sorry. This is like a disaster film, but this van is a lot smaller than the *Titanic*."

Gracie returned the embrace, then reached up front to squeeze Lester's shoulder. Her friend nodded as he handed Don his heavy leather gloves.

"Let's go," Don ordered. "The rest of you stay put! Don't anyone leave this van. Got that?"

Did they have a choice?

The door slammed shut. Gracie gasped as the frigid air bit into her skin. Steeling herself against the wind, she quickly pulled Barb's hat down over her ears and scrambled after Don.

She tried not to let her mind wander, concentrating only on maintaining her balance and attempting to step into Don's tracks.

Dear Father, help me help us. It's so dark and cold out here, and the snow is so high. We need Your protection, especially Uncle Miltie, Estelle and Lester. Please give Don the fortitude to lead us to safety and give me the strength to follow him. I know You are watching over us. I feel Your power and know You will not abandon us. For that I thank You and praise Your name. I just wish I wasn't so tired.

In some places, the snow was above her knees, and plowing on, it wasn't hard to lose track of time. First her nose burned, followed by her toes, and finally her fingers. At one point her boot caught and she flipped back with a startled cry. For a moment, she lay face up in the darkness, exhausted as the damp snow seeped into her pants. Her legs ached, her neck throbbed and she was afraid that her nose was already frostbitten.

As she stared up into the swirling flakes, a favorite verse from the Acts of the Apostles slipped into her mind. *And now behold, the hand of the Lord is upon thee: and thou shalt be blind, not seeing the sun for a time. And immediately there fell a mist and darkness upon him: and going about he sought someone to lead him by the hand.*

"Gracie?" Don shouted above the wind, his gloved hand reaching down to grasp hers. "You all right?"

She nodded and clambered to her feet. With a grim smile, she pushed him on into the dark and hip-high snow toward their destination.

"Yes?" a girlish voice called out tentatively from behind the heavy front door of a two-story clapboard farmhouse.

"Please!" Don shouted, shoving hard and partially opening the door. "We need help. Let us in."

"There's been an accident," Gracie added.

"But—" the girl protested, as they pushed inside into a dimly lit entrance. "Hey, wait! You can't just come barging—oh, Mr. Delano!"

"I'm sorry but—Bridget!" Gracie exclaimed, recognizing her. "Good heavens, child! What are you doing here?"

Hands covered by a pair of heavy men's gloves, Bridget Freeman tugged her oversized coat more tightly across her thin chest. "I live here."

Her brother, also swathed in bulky clothes and a wool cap, approached from another room, carrying a candle. With his other arm, he held the hand of a little girl who was wrapped in a thick blanket.

"Mrs. Parks, Mr. Delano—what are you doing here? What's happened?"

Gracie blinked. Though it wasn't all that warm, the snow on her eyelids and hat quickly began melting. "There's been an accident. We need your phone, dear. We've left our friends injured in a wrecked van that got knocked off the road."

"Where is the phone?" Don demanded. "We really can't lose any time."

Trent shook his head. "It's no use. The lines are down. The phone's out and has been for several hours."

"Where's your aunt?" Gracie asked. "We're going to need some help."

"At work," Bridget quickly replied.

"Visiting relatives," Trent said.

"Shopping," the small girl chimed in.

Don and Gracie exchanged a startled glance.

17

"S HE'S AT WORK," Bridget repeated firmly, shushing the younger two with a dark look. "She can't get home because of the storm." She quickly changed the subject. "What kind of help do you need?"

"We've left five people out there, three injured. We need some sort of sled to pull them here."

The little girl's eyes shone. "I've got one, don't I, Trent?"

The boy nodded. "I'll get my boots. I hope it's big enough."

"It will be," Bridget said confidently.

"Thank goodness," Gracie said. "But what about Trixie?"

"Oh, don't worry about her," Bridget said. "She's okay on her—" she hesitated.

"She'll be all right," Trent quickly added. "She knows not to touch the candles or the fire."

Trixie nodded. "It's okay. I've been alo—"

"Trixie!" her sister snapped. "Into the living room. Now! You'll catch a cold out here."

The little girl's face fell. "I'll be good. You'll see. I promised Santa." She turned and disappeared into the living room.

Don glanced at Gracie. "I think we'll have to risk it. They'll freeze out there if left much longer."

Gracie mentally ran through the difficult task ahead, then shook her head. "We're going to have to make two trips, anyway. There's no way that anyone with injuries can walk. And however large it is, I doubt we can pull more than two on a sled."

"I guess you're right," Don replied.

"So," Gracie continued, "someone—for the sake of argument, Barb, let's say—has got to stay behind in the van with, let's say, Lester. That leaves you, me and Marge taking turns pulling Estelle and Uncle Miltie."

"That sounds workable, but I think it would be better if we took Estelle or your uncle with Les."

Puzzled, Gracie looked at him.

Don shrugged. "He's smaller. He'll make a lighter load."

"What about us?" Trent demanded.

Gracie smiled down at him. "You've got to stay home with Trixie. Bridget can come with us."

"But why her?"

Don placed his hand on the boy's shoulder. "We're depending on you, son. To take care of your sister and to keep the fire burning. We're going to need it when we get back. Can I trust you?"

Trent nodded.

"Are there any extra blankets?" Gracie asked. "Rope?"

Bridget replied, "Just a sec."

She raced up the stairs and returned, her arms loaded with old blankets and a tattered sleeping bag. Trent ran down a hallway and came back with a coil of thick rope.

Don spied two backpacks hanging near the entrance. He rudely dumped their contents onto the floor. Gracie spied a familiar much-scrawled-upon envelope amid the stuff he left lying there.

This was definitely not the moment to get to the bottom of that puzzle. The important thing now was her friends.

"Quick, Trent. Stuff them in these."

The boy did as he was told.

Don slipped one of the packs over his shoulders, then handed the other to Gracie. She yanked it on as Don spoke. "Let's get a move on, then."

Gracie realized that Bridget had no scarf, so she carefully wrapped her own around the young woman's face. She couldn't help noticing that the smudges under Bridget's eyes were now darker, her face thinner. It took Trent half a minute to drag Trixie's sled to the front. Then, he and Trixie watched the small convoy tramp into the chilly darkness, each carefully stepping into the tracks of the one before.

It was a night none of them would soon forget, calling into

play a miracle of team work, endurance and faith. Buffeted by freezing winds, and hampered by waist-high drifts, the returning rescuers were soon disoriented in the middle of a field where their earlier tracks had vanished, swept away by the whistling snow. Gracie was whispering a prayer when Don Delano's sense of direction came to their rescue. Unfazed, he trudged on to the highway until they caught a glimmer of light and heard the muffled sound of voices, singing hoarsely.

It was coming from their van!

Don arrived first and yanked open the door. A bizarre mixture of bayberry and stale air assailed Gracie's nostrils.

The stranded quintet were huddled around a lighted, scented candle—one of Marge's gifts for her mom—mouths open, lips blue, bodies shaking.

Gracie nearly cried with relief.

"Iiiit's aaaboutt ttttime," Marge whispered, her teeth chattering uncontrollably. "We'ddd rrrruun ouuutttaa sssssongs aaandd ccccandddles sssooonn."

"Is everyone all right?" Gracie asked, poking her head inside. "Uncle Miltie?"

Her uncle's face was pale in the flickering light but he gave her a shaky thumbs-up.

"Estelle? Les?"

Marge, Estelle and Les, whose hands were shoved into a

pair of sheepskin slippers he had purchased for his father, nodded simultaneously.

Don pulled Gracie's head outside and shouted over the winds, unable to see through the fog on his glasses. "We can't leave anyone behind! We'll have to drag one of them on a blanket."

Gracie nodded. "It had better be Les. Marge and Barb can pull him." She dove back into the van and quickly told the others their action plan.

They managed to get Estelle and Uncle Miltie, each wrapped in a blanket, crammed onto the small wooden sled. Then Don and Gracie grabbed hold of the rope and, with a mighty effort, dragged. Nothing happened.

"Again!" Don shouted.

Gracie pulled until she thought her spine would crack, but the sled wouldn't budge. She ignored the stabbing pain in her neck.

"Please, God!" she whispered. "Give me the strength."

As Uncle Miltie and Estelle rocked on the sled, they heaved a third time. After a moment, the runners suddenly ripped across the crust, sliding easily over the icy clumps. With her arms and legs screaming, Gracie couldn't find the energy to celebrate.

In the meantime, Marge carefully assisted a hobbling Lester over to where Bridget and Barb struggled against the winds to flatten the sleeping bag on the ground. Once Les was down, Bridget wrapped the last blanket around his shoulders, then ran to catch up and help with the heavy sled. With Lester holding on to the edges of the sleeping bag, Marge wrapped the rope underneath his back and through his hands. Gripping the other end, she and Barb yanked with all their might.

Barb slipped, crashed onto the crusted snow. Marge hauled her to her feet, and Barb regained her hold. With Les yelling encouragement, both women forged ahead. Lester lurched, the sleeping bag sighed and then slipped along the surface. They hurried, stumbling often, trying to stay in the sled's path.

During the next twenty minutes, Gracie lost count of the number of times she wanted to give up and just sit down. But when she looked behind her, she found herself heartened by her friends' moving silhouettes. *Lord, to face an ordeal like this is to know that in loving teamwork we find the blessings of Your grace. Knowing that, I find strength where I thought there was none left.*

The throb in her neck was constant. But every time her legs weakened or her grip slipped, her eyes caught an expression from one of the others—Don's icy grimace, Bridget's determined gaze, her own uncle's encouraging smile—and she prayed for the strength for one more step, one more tug.

Finally, like the welcoming sound of a pealing church bell, Trixie's childish voice filled their ears.

"You made it!"

SOON THE WILLOW BEND TRAVELERS, tired but triumphant, were propped in front of the fire blazing from the glass door of the pot-bellied wood stove, which cast heat over only part of the large living room. The rest of the area remained in chilly darkness. By the light of a candle, Marge applied a bandage to Estelle's cut, using a first aid kit provided by Trent. Gracie rubbed her neck, then took her uncle's pulse. The others flopped onto a nearby couch and chairs, savoring the warmth from the stove.

"You're sure you're not having any more stomach pains?" Gracie asked Uncle Miltie.

"No. Now, stop worrying so much, dear. I'm getting my strength back, a little at a time."

"Trent, dear, how far is the closest neighbor?"

The teen stopped poking the fire. "About two miles."

Gracie shivered.

"Too far to walk," Don said. "Today, at any rate . . . after our last bit of exercise."

Several heads nodded vehemently.

"I'm not sure which part of me hurts the most," Lester declared, as Don gently examined his swollen ankle. "Ooww!"

"Sorry," Don replied. "Not broken, thank heavens. Just a sprain. The swelling's minimal. You can thank the cold for that. Hey, Trent? Mind going out to fill me a plastic bag with snow to use as an icepack?"

The boy nodded and headed for the door, accompanied by Trixie.

"I'm hungry," Trixie said softly, when she returned.

"Me, too, honey," Don added, gently raising Lester's injured leg to wrap the ice around his swollen joint.

"Me, three," Les agreed. "And I didn't even pull!"

Gracie willed her own trembling legs to stand. If she held her head a certain way, the pain was minimal. *Dearest God, I know You are ready to heal me. But I can't do anything but feel responsible for everyone else right now. So let me get back to You on that one!*

"Well, gang, it looks like we're going to be here for a while. Might as well make the best of it. Okay? Don? You and Trent fill that firebox and stoke the fire. Marge, Barb and I will go whip something up."

"Bridget!" Gracie called. "Do you mind showing us around?"

Each carrying a candle, the quartet trooped into the dark kitchen. As they left the protective shadow of warmth cast by the stove, Gracie shivered. Every time they spoke, a tiny cloud of condensation enveloped their words.

"It's awfully wintry back here," Marge said.

"I'm afraid we haven't been shopping for a while," Bridget said, pushing aside a pile of dirty dishes. "My aunt's been real busy."

"Oh, I'm sure we'll find something," Marge replied, confidently tugging open cupboards. "She's sure to keep a full larder, living way out here."

But shelf after shelf was bare.

"Empty!" Marge kept repeating.

"Nothing but a box of breakfast cereals and four packets of macaroni and cheese," Barb said. "There's not much in here either," she added, her head stuck into the freezer. "Couple of frozen pizzas and . . . wait a second . . ." There was a rustling noise as she rooted around. "Hey! Burritos. At least a dozen!"

"Whoopee," Marge said, leaning glumly against a counter and blowing on her hands.

"No eggs. No milk. Not even any bread!" Gracie exclaimed, closing the fridge. "Bridget, dear, where's all the food?"

"I told you," the girl replied. "My aunt's been busy." She stalked out of the kitchen.

The women regarded each other in the flickering light.

"Anyone ever cooked using a pot-bellied stove?" Marge asked.

"It can't be that hard," Gracie replied. "Maybe we can use the top like a range?" Barb nodded.

"I'm not sure how to handle the pizza," Marge said. "So let's try the burritos and the macaroni and cheese!"

Carrying a dozen burritos wrapped in aluminum foil and a metal saucepan of water, Marge and Gracie returned to their hungry friends. Don had added a couple of logs to the fire. "Don't have to worry about keeping warm," he said. "There's a fine supply of wood."

Gracie carefully slid the burritos into the glowing embers. "Just like the potatoes my mom used to make," commented Les.

As she waited for the water to boil, Gracie's eyes roamed the room. Though the light was poor, she was able to discern a number of things, all very puzzling. Clothes were piled in a heap in one corner, dirty dishes were in a jumble on the table and there were half-empty glasses on the floor. A batch of mail lay scattered on a nearby side table. Checking the water, Gracie sidled over and glanced down. Several of the envelopes were addressed to Harriet Kimball, some opened.

Something wasn't right. It nagged at her while she flipped the burritos and gauged the progress of the pot of water.

A number of incidents suddenly lined up in her head, like a tidy picket fence. She mentally ticked them off: Trent continually refusing to accept a ride home, Bridget's constant anxiety and exhaustion, Don's comment about Harriet Kimball's excessive neatness, the aunt herself never returning phone calls, the page of forged signa—

"Hey, I've got it!" Lester's voice interrupted her thoughts.

I KNEW I KNEW YOU," Lester crowed, jabbing a finger at Trent Freeman. "I remember *exactly* where we met!"

"Look, I told you," Trent replied. "We've *never* met."

Lester's eyes were dancing. "Oh, yes, we have." He shifted and winced momentarily. "You, young man, were hitching."

Trent's face paled.

"I picked you up just outside town and drove you right here. Well, to the end of the lane."

"Sorry. It must have been some other kid."

"Nope." Les pointed. "It was you, Trent."

"After Thanksgiving?" Gracie asked, adding the macaroni to the now boiling water.

Les nodded.

"But, Trent. Was that the first night you came?" Gracie wondered, looking at the boy, who was sitting on the couch between his sisters. "I offered you a ride and you told me you were meeting your aunt. Were you lying?"

Some undercurrent of communication flickered between Trent and Bridget.

"Oh," Bridget began, her tone strained. "That night!" She attempted a laugh. "What a mix-up that was, huh, Trent? Aunt Harriet got the time wrong, didn't she?"

Trent's face brightened. "Yeah. That's it. She got the time wrong. Aunt Harriet was long gone. I didn't want her to have to come all the way into town." He flashed a glance in Les's direction. "Guess I forgot."

"See?" Les said, beaming. "Even in my condition, the old noggin just keeps on ticking."

Don grinned. "Just so long as you remember to wind it."

A chuckle was heard from somewhere in the direction of Uncle Miltie.

"You shouldn't be hitchhiking, Trent," Don said. "You know better than that. You're lucky Les picked you up. Next time, it might be a different story."

"Yeah. Right," Trent said in a tight voice.

Gracie left to drain the macaroni over the sink. After she'd added the powdered cheese packet, she announced, "Soup's on! Get it while it's hot!"

Barb took a tentative bite. "Not bad."

"Okay, everyone!" Marge echoed her. "Grab a plate and come on over!"

While Marge spooned out macaroni and cheese, Gracie let Don carefully remove the wrapped burritos. Only a couple of edges were burned. It didn't take long to fill the plates and even less time for the assembled guests, along with their three hosts, to empty them.

"Hey! This is pretty good," Uncle Miltie exclaimed between chews.

"I love macaroni and cheese," Trixie told him, looking serious. "I love spaghetti, too."

"Don't talk with your mouth full," Trent scolded her, doing exactly the same thing.

Gracie approached her uncle. "How's the stomach?"

"It's fine." He shrugged sheepishly. "It's even possible I had one too many pieces of homemade divinity at the fair."

Gracie laughed and licked a bit of sticky cheese off her finger.

Estelle now looked a bit more like her normal self. "Just what the doctor ordered. Thanks."

Trixie yawned and leaned against her brother's shoulder. In a few seconds, she was asleep. Soon he was, as well.

Marge smiled and covered them in a blanket. "I'm getting a bit drowsy myself. Hey, Gracie, let's clean up before we collapse."

Uncle Miltie was already snoring. Bridget's eyes were shut. Don poked at the fire. Noticing the sleepers, he slipped in another large log, then shut the glass door quietly. The flames danced with renewed energy.

Gracie had found a blanket to lay over her uncle.

Barb poured water into the metal pot used to boil the macaroni, then placed it on the stove. "Now that we've had some food, let's see if we have the strength to wash a few dishes, or at least freshen them."

"Sorry I can't help you," Les said.

"Rest that ankle," Gracie replied. "We've got more than enough helping hands."

"Well, if you insist, I think I'll just close my—" His breathing slowed as he slipped into sleep.

By the time the water had boiled, those still awake were congregated in the kitchen, now a little less forbidding, thanks to a few strategically placed candles.

"Does anyone else think there's something odd going on here?" Marge asked.

Don hesitated. "You're suggesting. . . ."

"Well, for one thing, did you see the pile of dirty clothes over there in the corner?" This came from Gracie.

They all looked at her.

"Nope," Don said. "But that doesn't mean I shouldn't have noticed them."

"Well, there must be several weeks' worth of laundry," Gracie explained. "Not to mention the dirty dishes left all over the place."

Don slid a couple of plates into an upper cupboard. "Hey! Toaster pastries!" He handed the box over to Gracie. "Anyone else examine the pile of mail?" His face flushed slightly. "I know you're not supposed to look at other people's mail but . . ."

"I did," Gracie replied. "Half of it's unopened. A number of bills, and pretty old ones, at that—judging from the postmark."

"So, what's going on?" Barb demanded. "What's your theory?"

Gracie sighed. She was thinking hard and her conclusions were unsettling. "I've got an idea," she told them. "But it's pretty far out there."

Marge turned to her friend. "Out there or not, I think you've been worried about Trent and his sisters before now, that's for sure. But you're afraid of what you've figured out."

"It's my belief the aunt has left." *Marge knows me too well*, Gracie thought to herself.

No one spoke for a couple of seconds.

"Left?" Marge asked. "You mean as in *flown the coop*?"

"Well," Gracie replied, "you said yourself that something was odd. I think Harriet Kimball abandoned these children. The evidence was in front of me, but I kept resisting my intuition. However, when you come right down to it, this is more than odd—it's criminal!"

Don whistled softly. "Wow."

"I can't believe it," Barb put in. "What woman could abandon three children?"

There was shocked silence.

"Well, if you're right, Gracie, and these kids are on their own," Marge said, shivering, "what are we going to do?"

"I'm not sure," Gracie answered. She offered up a silent prayer. "But I know Who I'm going to ask for guidance."

20

IN THE DIM LIGHT, the four friends joined hands. Gracie began reciting the *Prayer of St. Francis*. Soon, the others joined in, and they recited the last few lines as one. "For it is in giving that we receive. It is in pardoning that we are pardoned. And it is in dying that we are born to eternal life. Amen."

Don added, "Dear Lord, thank You for protecting and saving us this day. Without Your watchful eye, I'm certain the accident and our injuries would have been much worse."

Marge continued. "And thank You for helping us find safety and warmth in this farmhouse. It surely was a miracle."

It was Barb's turn. "Oh, heavenly Father, I, too, am very blessed to have had Your protection. I'm sure our families and friends are very worried about us. If You could somehow let them know that we're all right, I'd be grateful. Thank You."

Gracie smiled. "Please, dear God, guide and help us to do what's right for the Freeman children." She almost added something that had crossed her mind when she first saw Bridget open the front door, but she stopped. She wanted to think about it a little longer. "Amen."

"Amen," repeated the others.

"*Psst!*" It was Lester, from the other room. "What's a guy have to do for a cup of coffee?"

Gracie and her companions grinned at one another.

"Sing a tune," Marge replied softly.

"Too loud," Les whispered. "I'll wake the kids."

"Dance a jig," Don said.

"With this bum ankle?"

Uncle Miltie's eyes opened. "Tell a joke?"

"That's your department."

"Enough!" Barb whispered, suppressing a laugh. "I'll boil some water."

As they gathered by Les to share the stale pastries— toasted on forks made of bent wire hangers—the Freeman kids slept soundly.

"*Hmm*, strawberry." Les took a bite. "My favorite, even if it's stale."

"So?" Don asked, cautiously sipping his too-weak instant coffee. "What are we going to do?"

"About what?" Estelle demanded. She sniffed. "Got any more of those?"

Don slid one onto a plate and handed it over. He pointed toward Trent and his sisters. In a low voice, he said, "We think they've been abandoned by their aunt."

Estelle's eyes grew wide. "Wha—"

"Sssshh!" the others hissed. "Don't wake them."

"I'll have to tell Bud," Don said. "That's what the teachers' guidelines say. I have no choice. The principal has to be informed about this situation."

He looked at his friends gravely. Barb nodded. Les was shaking his head slowly.

"But that will mean the county will have to get involved. And social workers. Won't they break them up until they decide what to do?" Gracie asked anxiously. "Put them in different homes?"

"They have their rules, that's all I know."

"Why can't you folks leave sleeping dogs lie?" asked Uncle Miltie. "Once bureaucrats, even kindly minded ones, step in, all kinds of things could happen. None of 'em good, if you ask me."

"But we can't just let them continue on their own," Marge reminded him.

"Why not?" the old man countered. "They're doing all right, aren't they?" He hesitated. "Well, keeping house isn't the most important thing. Look at them."

All eyes stared at the youngsters, their unlined faces glowing in the firelight. Like a cozily nesting kitten, Trixie had rested her head against Trent's shoulder and her hand on her sister's leg.

"They're together. Don't you see? That's what matters."

"I agree with my uncle," Gracie said, hoping she was doing the right thing. "They mustn't be separated." She thought for a moment and seemed to feel the Lord's hand on her own shoulder, setting her in the proper direction.

She continued, her voice low and steady. "Here we are, planning to raise money for a needy local family while we have one right in front of our very eyes! And not only that! That boy's been in my house and I didn't manage to figure out the signals that he needed help!"

Marge patted her on the arm. "None of us knew. The kids were pretty good at covering their tracks."

"Maybe," Gracie said. "I know I was listening, I just wasn't hearing."

"Does anybody know how old Bridget is?" Estelle asked.

The others shook their heads.

"Sixteen? Seventeen?" Don offered.

Estelle shifted in her chair. A paper fluttered to the ground, but it was Don who reached down to get it. "Soon she'll be considered an adult and capable of taking care of others. That's got to be considered."

"But," Marge said, "right this minute, she's still too young." She sighed. "It's really too bad. They've tried so hard."

"Listen to this!" Don interrupted, holding up a piece of paper. "One jeweled crown, preferably gold; a staff; two yards of purple satin—hey!" he cried, as Marge took the paper from his hands.

"Sorry, but I know what it's about," she said, reading quickly. "It's for the pageant. I helped Pat send the letters out. It's a description for a costume. One of the three kings, I think. Must be for Trixie," she added, glancing quickly at the sleeping child. "Someone's written in the margins." She showed the letter to Gracie. "See? There's a dollar amount beside each item."

Gracie understood. "That's why he asked me how much two yards of purple satin cost!"

"Who?" Uncle Miltie demanded.

"Trent. He wouldn't explain but . . ." Marge held out the letter.

"My name's on the bottom," Gracie exclaimed, taking the paper. "Yours too, Marge. And the Finkmeyers and old Mrs. Martin. I wonder why?"

"That's easy," said Uncle Miltie. "He's been shoveling all your driveways."

"Of course!" Gracie exclaimed. "So . . . this is what the money's for."

"Let me see that," Uncle Miltie asked. He examined the letter for a moment. "He's short a few dollars, poor kid."

Estelle and Lester both looked contemplative. Then a twinkle entered Les's eyes. He reached into his wallet and pulled out a five-dollar bill. "Stuff this into his jacket," he said, motioning to Don. "He'll never know."

The chemistry teacher added the same amount and shoved the bills into Trent's jacket.

For a few minutes, the soft sighs and moans of the sleeping children were the only sounds in the room.

Well, dear Lord? I hope I'm correct and that what I'm about to say pleases You. I've thought about it for a long time, always sensing Your encouragement. Your presence fills me with confidence. I thank You, Father, for Your unyielding trust, for allowing me to be an instrument of Your love.

The time was right for Gracie to air what had been on her mind when they'd first arrived, when she'd seen Bridget open the door. "I've got a confession," Gracie finally said.

Their faces registering surprise, her friends turned to her.

"You may think I'm crazy but . . . I don't think today was an accident."

"What do you mean?" Don snapped, his tone defensive. "That truck swerved right in front of us. There wasn't any time—"

Gracie patted his arm. "No, no. *That* was an accident, Don.

You saved our lives, of that I have no doubt. What I meant is that our being here isn't an accident."

Barb frowned. "You mean, the whole thing was planned?"

"But hhhow?" Estelle stammered. "No one could have predicted this."

A smile played across Marge's lips. "No one *human*, you mean. Right, Gracie?"

Gracie laughed softly. "I think we were brought here on purpose, my friends. To help these dear children."

Uncle Miltie slapped his knee. "Well, I'll be darned. Good for you, Gracie. Good for you."

Bridget stirred.

Lester pursed his lips. "Well, if that's the case, Don, you'd better tell us what you know about what will happen after you tell Bud. I imagine he'll get in touch with the Family Services caseworkers . . . ."

"What!" Bridget shrieked, leaping off the couch. "Family Services! No! No way!"

BRIDGET WENT FROM THE PLACIDITY of sleep to near hysteria in only an instant. "I told you! I told you! No one ever believes me. But I didn't steal that old woman's bracelet! I didn't! I didn't! You can't say I did!"

Startled by the noise, Trixie began bawling.

Suddenly, everyone else was scrambling to their feet. In her haste to rise, Estelle knocked over a candle. As the yellow stick flipped end over end, droplets of hot wax flew, striking Les and Uncle Miltie. "Ouch!" they yelled simultaneously.

Don then jumped over Les, grabbed the candle off the carpet and blew it out. All the while, Bridget was alternatively shouting and weeping, warning Trent and Trixie of their impending separation. Gracie's arms were around Trixie, hugging tightly. She was attempting to soothe her, but the little girl was inconsolable. She reached out for Bridget.

"GET OUT OF OUR HOUSE!" they suddenly heard. "NOW!"

There was an odd click.

Shivers snaked up Gracie's neck.

Trent Freeman had stepped out of the shadows. Something metallic glinted in the firelight.

Gracie blinked, unable to believe her eyes.

In his trembling fingers, the boy cradled a shotgun.

His voice cracking, Trent repeated, "I said, *get out of our house*."

"Whoa, son!" Don cried.

"Trent, dear," Gracie murmured in a soothing voice. "Put that down."

Barb put her hand across her mouth as she fought back a gasp of fright.

The boy's grip tightened.

"He's going to kill us!" Estelle moaned. "Oh, dear heavens, he's going to kill us!" Her eyes rolled upward and she fell onto her chair in a dead faint.

Barb couldn't hold back any longer. Hugging her arms to chest, she let out a frightened cry.

Marge and Gracie ran to Estelle. With Don's help, they managed to drag her upright as Marge began slapping her hand.

"Bridget! Trixie! Over here!" Trent commanded.

The girls raced to his side. Trent pushed Trixie behind his

back. "Nobody's ever going to split us up. Nobody!" He swung the shotgun back and forth. "You got that?"

"Now, Trent," Don started. "Let's just calm down—"

"Don't tell him what to do!" Bridget snapped. "You grown-ups are *always* telling us what to do. But we're doing fine, just fine, without you." She picked up the sobbing Trixie and cuddled her protectively.

"That's right," Trent said. "And we're going to do even better when you're gone. Which is right now!"

Gracie saw a meaningful look slip between Lester and Don. She desperately tried to keep the boy's attention. "Trent! Trent! Listen to me. Put that gun away." She took a step toward the trio of children. Trent's eyes locked onto hers and he pointed the weapon. Behind Gracie, Marge muffled a gasp. "There's no need for violence," Gracie continued, her voice suddenly soft. "It won't solve anything. It'll just make things worse. Now, listen to me. Listen! No one's trying to hurt you or split you up. No one!"

Uncle Miltie spoke for the first time. "That gun looks older than me, boy. I'll bet you the bullets for it no longer exist, do they?"

"Do you want to find out?" Trent snapped, whirling toward Gracie's uncle.

Lester suddenly began groaning. Loudly.

Trent's eyes momentarily flicked in his direction.

"Oowww!" Les wailed, pointing dramatically. "My ankle! Help me, please. It feels like it's on fire!" He writhed back and forth, his distress escalating in intensity.

All three children stared at him, uncertain how to react.

Estelle opened her eyes. "What happened?"

"Somebody help me!" Les cried. "Please! It hurts too much!"

Trixie started to cry.

There was a movement behind the kids.

Estelle snapped forward, a protest rising in her throat.

Trent whirled, but not in time.

Don Delano roughly yanked the shotgun out of the boy's hands.

THE ROOM WAS SUDDENLY COOL, the embers dying slowly in the belly of the stove.

"It wasn't loaded," Trent confessed. "Uncle Miltie was right."

Trixie howled as Bridget stumbled back, almost dropping her.

"I'm not going to hurt you," Don reassured them. He broke the gun's breach, peered inside the bullet chamber, then nodded to the others.

"It's all right," Gracie said. "It's all over now."

"I . . . I never meant to hurt anyone," Trent said, sobbing. "Honest. But . . . but they're my sisters." A tear rolled down his freckled cheek. "I promised my mom before . . ." He gulped. "I have to protect them, don't I?"

Gracie put her arm around him, touched by typically adolescent mixture of vulnerability and volatility. "Of course you do. But violence isn't necessary. Come and sit down." She looked at the two girls. "All of you."

"Yes," Marge added, reaching for Trixie's hand. "We'll talk, figure this out. Give her to me, Bridget."

The little girl tentatively touched Marge's fingers before allowing herself to be taken.

"I heard you," Bridget said, defiantly crossing her arms. "You said Family Services. You're going to try and pin that robbery on me. Then use that as an excuse to split us up!"

Gracie sighed. "No, dear. No one's going to *pin* anything on anyone. My goodness, you sound like you're in a detective story. As I told you before, they're not even sure the bracelet's been stolen. Now, come and sit down."

"Come on!" Uncle Miltie added encouragingly. "It can't be as bad as all that."

Reluctantly, the three returned to the fire. Trent helped Don choose the wood and soon the flames leapt again. The kids huddled together on the couch.

"Now, tell us about your aunt," Gracie began.

Bridget and Trent exchanged a glance. "Girls first," he said, suddenly shy.

Bridget stared at Gracie for a moment. "She's great," she started, her tone obviously forced. "She came to live with us after our mom . . . uh . . . ," she said, glancing at her little sister, ". . . passed away last year."

"If she's so great," Marge asked, "why isn't she here?"

Bridget's eyes flashed. "I told you. She's stuck at work."

Trent clenched his fists.

"When was the last time she was here?" Gracie asked. Her tone was friendly, her manner patient.

"Duh! She's here *all* the time. She *lives* here."

"Calm down, Bridget," Don admonished her gently. "She's not here now."

She flushed. Trent's back stiffened.

"For heavens' sake, you kids!" Marge broke in. "Don told us your friends called your aunt a neat freak." She stretched out her arms, pointing to the disarray surrounding them. "My guess is she's been away for a long time."

"No, she hasn't!" Trent retorted.

"Bridget," Gracie began. "Listen to us. We'd like to help you, but we can't if you continue this ridiculous charade." Gracie could see that the young woman was trembling, near tears. "I know what you're trying to do. Your mother would be very proud of you. Of all of you. But . . . look at yourself, dear. You're still in school, trying to run a house *and* take care of your siblings. Plus, you have a job. It's too much."

Bridget's lower lip quivered. In the flickering light, she suddenly looked very frail.

"We can take care of ourselves!" Trent protested, now near tears himself.

Gracie smiled gently. "You're both worn out. There's no

food in the house, Trixie hasn't had a bath in days, your brother wears the same clothes day in and day out. It's not supposed to be like this. We can help. If you'll let us."

Trent's voice was steady again. "We don't need your help."

"I think you do."

Then, Bridget sighed, as though coming to a difficult decision. "All right," she said, her voice sounding thick with relief. "No, Trent! It's, it's over. We . . . I can't . . ." She caught her breath. "It's too much, Mrs. Parks. I need help . . . I'm just so tired. . . ."

Gracie leaned out to stroke her hair. With a sob, the teenager pressed her face against Gracie's chest.

"Bridgie, don't cry!" Trixie leapt off Marge's lap and flung herself at her sister.

Gracie hugged them both. "It'll be all right," she repeated soothingly. Trent stared into the fire, his shoulders slumped. Silently, the others watched.

After a while, Bridget pushed away, slightly embarrassed. "I . . . I don't know what to say." Trixie slid off Gracie's lap and went to hug her brother to comfort him.

"What happened to your aunt?" Don asked. "Has she abandoned you?"

Trent opened his mouth, but Bridget held up a weary hand. "Forget it, Trent. She's gone to care for our other aunt, who has cancer."

"How long has she been gone?"

Bridget paused. "About two months, I guess."

"Two months!" Barb echoed.

"It's better without her," Trent offered. "Much better."

Gracie asked the question on all their lips. "Why?"

"She's mean!" The youth's eyes flashed. "From the day she arrived, she kept telling us how she never wanted us. How we were a such a *burden*. She wouldn't let us play with our friends. We had to stay home and clean!" He bit off a laugh. "You won't believe it, but you could have eaten off this floor."

"I did," Trixie said.

The adults smiled.

"We tried, at first," Bridget added. "We really did. But Aunt Harriet was *never* satisfied. *Ever!* 'You can do better than that,'" she crooned, in a singsong voice. "'Clean it again. And again.'"

"'Until it shines!'" the three children shouted simultaneously.

"Then what happened?" Estelle asked.

"Well, it was pretty rough. There were a lot of fights." Bridget looked disdainfully at her brother. "Trent kept coming home late. His grades dropped. That made things worse. A *lot* worse."

"She didn't even like it when I hung out with my friends," Trent said, remembering.

Bridget rolled her eyes. "Then, Aunt Harriet got a call from the doctor, who said Aunt Bess needed her."

"She was glad to go," Trent declared. "She was!"

Bridget continued, "My . . . our mom had given me a bankbook in my name. She told me the money was for emergencies only. I hadn't even *looked* in it until . . . well, when Aunt Harriet said she might have to leave, I looked."

Trent's eyes shone. "A thousand dollars!"

His older sister nodded. "So, I figured we'd be okay without her. I encouraged her to go, said we'd be fine on our own."

"And we are!" Trent added.

"She . . . she just *left* you?" Marge asked, her mouth dropping open.

"She said it was history repeating itself," Bridget explained. "She kept telling us how she—"

Trent interrupted, voicing one word. "'Singlehandedly.'"

A grin flashed across Bridget's face, momentarily dashing away the fears and fatigue. "Right. How she *singlehandedly* raised our mom and Aunt Bess. And so when she was gone, we did okay on our own, too. We had each other, the house and money."

Her brother nodded vehemently. "Then, a few days later when she called to say she would have to stay longer, I told her that we were fine and not to hurry back."

"She hasn't been here since?" Barb asked.

They shook their heads.

"Everything's been going just fine," Trent said emphatically.

Gracie watched his sister's face darken with a frown. She took a shot. "So why were you practicing your aunt's signature?"

Trent's head snapped up. "What? How'd you—"

"Quiet!" his older sister cried.

"Everything's fine, is it, Bridget?"

The girl sighed. "I knew we needed help, but I couldn't bear to have someone break us up." Her voice rose. "And they're not going to, are they?"

"Child," Gracie said, "listen to me. I'm sure there's a way. You're running out of money, aren't you?"

Bridget nodded. "At first, I ignored the bills. But then the gas company called, asking to see my aunt about a late payment. I didn't want them cutting us off, so, I had to pay it. It pretty well wiped us out."

Trent sprinted over to the table and grabbed the mail. "There's county assistance money that comes in—but it's in her name. So . . ."

"You were going to forge your aunt's signature and cash the checks?" Don asked.

Trent held up his head. "It's not fair! It's *our* money," he replied. "It should be in our names, anyway." He ripped out a check and shoved it at Gracie. "See, Mrs. Parks? This proves my sister didn't steal that stupid bracelet. We wouldn't be trying to cash these if she had."

Gracie looked at Bridget. The girl had denied stealing the bracelet more than once. Why? *The lady doth protest too much*, Gracie thought, her high-school knowledge of *Hamlet* suddenly returning.

Bridget lowered her eyes.

"You know *something* about Mrs. Simmons's bracelet. Don't you, Bridget? But what?"

NO!" BRIDGET ANSWERED QUICKLY—but anxiety shadowed her face, nonetheless.

"Leave her alone!" Trent shouted, rushing to his sister's side. "She didn't do anything wrong!"

"Quiet!" his sister warned him. "I've told you, it's nothing for *you* to worry about."

Gracie was about to question them further when Trixie's whimpers of fear silenced the room.

The little girl ran to her sister and hugged her legs. "I want my mama!" she cried. "I want my mama back!"

While Trixie sobbed as though her heart would break, the adults looked at one another. Their own woes were forgotten.

"There, there," Barb said, her voice soft. "It's going to be all right."

"You're overtired, little one," Gracie said. "Why don't you lie back down on the couch? I'll tell you stories about my big, funny cat...."

The crying just grew worse. Tears streaming down her own cheeks, Bridget held the inconsolable Trixie and stroked her hair. Trent stood at their side, defiance and woe mixed on his thin face.

"Forget cats, I'll bet you haven't seen Santa," Uncle Miltie tried. "Well . . ." he paused dramatically when the sobbing subsided slightly. "I've seen the jolly old elf himself."

Trixie rubbed away the tears. "You've *seen* Santa Claus?"

Gracie tried to catch her uncle's eye, but the older man was gazing intently at the little girl.

Uncle Miltie nodded.

Trixie slowly walked over to his chair while the others watched, holding their breath.

"What's he really look like?" she asked, eyes glowing in the firelight.

Gracie's uncle grinned. "What do *you* think?" He patted his lap.

Without hesitation, Trixie climbed up and nestled in the crook of his arm. "He's probably fat, like all the pictures of him. He likes to eat pizza, I know, whenever he leaves the North Pole, because they don't make it up there. But are those the only reindeer he has? Don't they get tired?"

Uncle Miltie winked at Trixie. "He's been trying out a second team, he told me. He's thinking of setting up a second workshop, too, right here in Indiana. Doesn't this weather remind you of the North Pole?"

Gracie caught Marge's eye and then glanced toward the

kitchen. They sneaked off as their friends were chuckling at Uncle Miltie's nonsense. Trixie was entranced.

"Whew!" Marge exclaimed. "That was close. I thought she was going to cry all night."

Gracie nodded. "Hey! Look what I just found." She handed Marge a cellophane-wrapped pouch.

"Popcorn!" Marge paused, eyeing Gracie carefully. "Hey, you okay? You're holding your neck funny."

Carefully, Gracie nodded. She did a few neck stretches to test her flexibility. "Ugh!" Followed by: "I think it's a good thing I *feel* something!"

The corn popped, sending a cheerful aroma through the room, and soon everyone was munching and sharing stories of their favorite Christmas Eve. Trent lay in front of the fire while his younger sister relaxed comfortably in Uncle Miltie's lap, listening intently.

An hour passed quickly. Finally, Don rose and fed the fire. The wood burst into a reassuring tattoo of flames.

Gracie noticed that Trixie had fallen asleep in her uncle's arms. He grinned at his niece, then closed his own eyes.

Bridget yawned, joined her brother and curled up on one of the blankets in front of the fire. She was breathing deeply in seconds. Trent pulled himself into a chair, folded his arms and stared into the flickering light. His head drooped and soon he had nodded off.

"They're awfully cute," Marge whispered, yawning. "Just like little angels."

Barb stretched. "More devilish, from what we've learned. Don't you think? Lying, forging signatures, maybe even stealing Mrs. Simmons's bracelet, for all we know."

Uncle Miltie's eyes fluttered open. "Maybe, maybe not, but remember what Plato said."

"Plato?" Marge said, her jaw dropping in astonishment.

Gracie's uncle blushed. "I had a history teacher once who loved to quote Greek philosophy."

"What did Plato say?" Estelle asked.

"*Be kind,*" Uncle Miltie started. *"For everyone you meet is fighting a hard battle."*

"They're just children, remember," Gracie added. "They can still be molded into good, productive human beings with a little effort and love."

Her uncle smiled at her. "That's right, dear. Just like clay."

"Thanks for reminding me."

The adults silently observed the sleeping children.

Thank You, dear Lord, for bringing these sweet children into our lives. Their struggle and dependence remind me of all our human fragility and that we, as Your children, must listen to Your wise words. I am reminded, too, how we must love and protect one another in Your holy name—for without You, there is no light, no hope and nothing to sustain us.

Gracie gently laid a blanket over Trent. "They're angels, all right. Just a little secretive."

THE POUNDING JERKED GRACIE AWAKE. It was dawn. The room was smoky and cold, the fire down to orange embers and faintly glowing ashes. Some dirty mugs and plates remained, scattered about the room, ignored the night before when the adults finally had surrendered to sleep. She moved, then gasped. Her neck throbbed.

The others groaned awake. Uncle Miltie muttered, "What's that noise?"

The heavy thumping began again, this time accompanied by a muffled bellow.

"Someone's at the door!" Bridget cried, bolting upright.

Trent beat her to it. Without warning, he yanked open the front door. A large, shivering man tumbled inside, barely able to keep his footing.

"Rocky!" Gracie cried, recognizing her friend buried underneath a sheepskin hat, wildly colored scarf and down jacket, all covered in ice crystals.

Rocky put his gloved hand to his frozen scarf. He opened his mouth, but his teeth chattered nearly too much to speak. He stomped his feet. "Gggracie?" He glimpsed the others. "Wwwwhat're you all ddddoing here?"

"Same thing as you," Don said, helping him remove his coat. "Finding shelter. Trent! Get that fire going. Somebody mind boiling some water for coffee?"

As Rocky began to thaw out, Gracie and Don took turns telling him about their accident. But he held up his hand. "We can swap stories as soon as I'm dry. First things first."

"Dear me!" Gracie exclaimed in alarm. She examined his wind-burned face for signs of frostbite. "You're right, of course. You've got to get out of those wet trousers!"

"Come on, Bridget," Marge commanded. "Let's see if we can find something he can wear."

"I'll give you a hand," Barb said, following them up the stairs.

"Where'd you come from?" Uncle Miltie asked.

"Spent half the night in my car." He shivered violently. "I hit a patch of ice. Then the tire blew."

Estelle returned, plunking the kettle onto the stovetop. "The coffee will be ready in a jiffy."

"Thanks."

"Hey!" Les called to Rocky. "Have you got your cell phone?"

They all looked at him expectantly.

The big man sighed. "Forgot it at the office."

There was a collective groan.

"I know. I know. Been kicking myself all night."

"Here you go," Marge said, stepping down the stairs. She handed Rocky an old pair of denim overalls.

"Thanks."

"Coffee anyone?" Estelle asked, tipping sparing measures into a half dozen mugs.

"Me!" Lester shouted.

Uncle Miltie shuffled over, took a filled mug, stirred, then handed it to Les. "How's the ankle?"

Les accepted it with a nod of thanks. "Not bad. Long as I don't put any weight on it. I've had sprains before. It'll be fine in a couple of days."

Gracie in turn gave her uncle a mug, then started sipping her own. Though not a coffee aficionada, and certainly not one who ever took it black, Gracie was astonished at how wonderful the bitter, pale brown instant coffee tasted. Her stomach growled. She remembered something her mother always said when Gracie and her siblings were unenthusiastic about a meal. "The difference between good food and bad food is three days without food." She smiled to herself, thinking how she'd eat practically anything at this moment. "Anybody hungry?"

"Is this the Hoosier State?" Rocky replied, returning and taking a bow in his new outfit.

Gracie stifled a giggle, desperate to avoid Barb's eye. It didn't matter. The choir director took a deep breath. Lester and Uncle Miltie gave up on any attempt at politeness and simply roared with laughter.

With his tousled hat-hair, day-old bristles and too-short overalls, the owner and editor of the *Mason County Gazette* looked like a refugee from the Grand Ole Opry.

"What?" he said, looking at himself. "Not my color?"

Gracie grinned and took his arm. "Handsome as always. Now, come and sit by the wood stove while we try to improvise some breakfast."

"Barb and I will do that, Gracie," Marge said. "You keep Rocky company."

While Trent and Don gathered in a fresh load of wood, Gracie quietly revealed to Rocky the Freeman children's unusual predicament.

Rocky listened patiently. After she'd finished, he sighed and reached forward to warm his fingers. "I don't know too much about child welfare. Sue Jameson, my features editor, she'd know more. She wrote a story about kids in foster care a while back."

Gracie heard her friends' voices floating in from the kitchen.

"How old is Bridget?" Rocky looked thoughtful.

"Seventeen, I think."

"Not quite legal age," he told her.

"I know."

They sat companionably in silence while Gracie examined the situation and its possible solutions.

She said, half to herself, "I just don't know! I'll do anything in my power to see these kids remain together. But I fear the law won't see it my way."

He stared at her with fond exasperation. "You're taking this personally, aren't you?"

She nodded sadly.

"Knowing you, Gracie, I probably shouldn't ask," he said. "But I have to. Why?"

"You may not understand or even believe," she replied quickly, "but the Lord asked me to." He shook his head, but the gesture was still fond.

"Do you think they'll be having a service this morning?" Estelle broke in, carrying another pot of water.

"Pastor Paul will be preaching to only the hardiest souls," Don replied, carefully stacking a pile of split wood on the floor by the stove.

"How about our own breakfast prayer?" Barb suggested.

Her fellow choir members nodded and bowed their heads. The children glanced awkwardly at one another, then Trent shrugged and glanced down. Trixie clasped her hands together.

"Uncle Miltie?" Don asked. "Would you please do the honor?"

The elderly man nodded slightly, cleared his throat, then began, "Bless us, oh Lord, for these Thy gifts which we are about to receive through Thy bounty and Christ our Lord. Amen." He bowed his head for a moment, then continued, "And please, bless our friends and relatives back in Willow Bend. Give them strength and courage while they await news of our whereabouts. Thank You for our safe haven and good health." He glanced down at Trixie. "And finally, bless these three children, whom You've brought into our lives. May their futures be as bright as the Christmas star. Amen."

"Amen," the others chorused.

"Lovely," Marge said.

"Really nice, Uncle Miltie," Lester added.

Rocky looked from the stove to Gracie, his face wrinkling with amusement. "My kind of breakfast! Is that a bowl with some popcorn kernels in it I see?"

She handed him the dish containing a forgotten few barely popped corns. "Crunch away. Just don't ask for a movie to go with it."

The hours crept by, punctuated by snatches of song as Barb attempted to entertain the increasingly fidgety Trixie. Rocky claimed the couch and, snoring softly, grabbed some much needed sleep. Tucked around the dining table, Marge held forth on the latest make-up fads.

"We're doing okay so far, don't you think?" Les asked, dragging himself into the chair beside Gracie.

She smiled. "Like a scene from a Currier and Ives picture."

"What are you going to do about the kids?"

Gracie stared at the flames, suddenly aware of the ache in her neck. "Why do you automatically assume that *I'm* the one to do something?"

"Gosh, Gracie, you know I didn't mean anything—it's just that . . . well, you know we count on you, Gracie. To lead us and help us do what's right." He paused, rubbing his ankle.

"Is it really painful?"

Les shook his head. "Look, what I'm trying to say is . . . well, I know you believe God stranded us here to help these kids. And seeing your face when you talked about it, so do I. And we'll all help. But, Gracie," his voice dropped to a whisper, "*you're* the one He was talking to. The rest of us are just along for the ride."

25

"YOU HOO!" a muffled voice bellowed. "Anybody home?"

"Oh my!" Estelle cried, so startled that her coffee mug tumbled from her fingers.

Before anyone could move, someone banged heavily on the front door. Another deeper voice sang out. "Hey! Gracie? Don? Les? You guys in there?"

This time, Bridget was first to the door, opening it quickly to reveal two faces partially hidden by ice-encrusted scarves. Seeing Bridget, both men blinked. "Uh, sorry," Rick Harding said. "We were looking for—" his dark eyes roamed past her and widened in delight as he saw his friends. "Gracie! Barb! Everybody! Thank God you're all here."

"We've been worried sick!" the other man cried.

"Rick!" Gracie shouted with joy. "Paul!"

"Is everyone all right?" Paul asked, glancing anxiously from face to face.

"Just minor injuries, thank goodness," Les answered, hobbling back to a chair.

"Did you hurt your ankle?"

"No big deal. How'd you find us?"

"Well," Rick started, shedding his heavy coat. "Comfort and I began to worry about you when the snow started coming down in drifts. We knew where you'd gone and the route you'd take home. After we heard on the news how dangerous the highways were we started calling each of you, to see if you'd gotten home safely."

Paul tugged off his boots. "Comfort phoned me in a panic after supper to tell me not one of you had made it home. Then, we took turns calling—but by nine, I decided to phone Herb. He told me it was all but impassable out there and that there was nothing anyone could do until the storm abated." Paul smiled softly. "He was wrong. We prayed, didn't we, Rick?"

Rick nodded vehemently, scattering droplets of water. "It was a long night, let me tell you." He yawned and settled into a chair near the pot-bellied stove. "When the roads opened early this afternoon, we came looking. Saw a small black car first and next the abandoned van. Paul spied Uncle Miltie's walker in the back . . ." he paused, his expression suddenly serious. "And the damage. Then we noticed this farmhouse and prayed again that you'd made it."

"Thank the good Lord, you did," Paul said. He stepped nearer the stove to warm his hands.

Noticing the half-awake newspaperman for the first time, Paul added, "Rocky!" Then he thought. "Oh! That little black sedan!"

Rocky stretched. "Spent part of the night in it."

"Guess someone above was watching over you, too," Rick said.

Rocky shrugged. "I can't argue with that."

Gracie smiled.

"Hey! Where are our manners?" Don asked. "You haven't met our hosts." He started to introduce them to the Freeman children. "Oh. Of course, you both met Trent at the pie bee—"

"No introductions necessary," interrupted the young pastor. "We're old friends."

"Right. Well then, Rick Harding, meet Bridget and Trixie Freeman."

Rick stood and smiled broadly at the youngsters.

"Coffee?" Estelle asked, holding two steaming mugs. "It's weak, but it's hot." The men gratefully accepted.

"Phone's still out?" Rick asked.

Don nodded. "I checked for the umpteenth time just a few minutes ago."

"The lines are down all over the county," Paul said. "It's going to be a while before services are restored." He leaned back, eyeing the flames. "This is nice. Very relaxing. Must have been a pretty boring night, once you folks got settled."

Barb inhaled sharply. Gracie exchanged an amused look with Marge. The two older Freemans looked sheepish while Trixie giggled.

It was up to Don Delano to say, "Depends on your definition of boring." He paused a beat. "Wouldn't you say, gang?" The room pealed suddenly with the joyous sounds of their laugher.

Astonished, Paul and Rick looked at one another.

"I don't get it," Paul finally blurted when he could be heard. "You *weren't* bored?"

That cracked them up all over again.

During a discussion of the logistics of moving Lester and Uncle Miltie down the snow-clogged lane, Gracie took Rick and the pastor aside and brought them into the picture. "So, you see," she said, finishing quickly. "We can't leave them here alone."

Paul nodded. "Where will we take them?"

"We've got that all worked out. Trent's going to stay with me while Marge puts up the two girls. That way they'll be close together and under adult supervision."

"And what about the authorities?" Rick asked.

"We're working on it," Gracie said. She glanced back. Trent

and Trixie were busy putting a puzzle together while Bridget listened to Marge. "But keep your voice down, please."

The two men gazed at her in surprise.

"Trust me. We've got some sensitive issues here."

"Sure," Rick replied immediately.

"All right, everybody!" Don shouted. "Attention!"

All eyes fixed on the young science teacher.

"This is what's going to happen. Rick, Paul and I will pull the sleigh carrying Les and Uncle Miltie and—"

"Me, too!" piped in Trixie.

Don grinned. "Okay. Now, the rest of you will follow us to the highway." He glanced at Rocky. "How far is your car from there?"

"Quarter of a mile, maybe. But it could really be socked in by now."

"We'll see. Rick needs to stay with the main group to drive the van. It will hold the three on the sleigh—"

"Hey!" Trent shouted. "This is our home. Remember? We're not going any where. Right, Bridgie?"

Bridget remained silent, biting her lower lip.

Gracie moved to his side. "You're all coming with us, Trent. You know we can't leave you alone. Not anymore."

Trent stumbled back. "But . . . but . . . it's not fair! We told you. We're doing just fine"

Trixie wailed and launched herself at her sister. "Come

on, Bridget," Trent pleaded. "Tell 'em! They'll split us up!"

The teenager clutched her sister tightly and slowly shook her head. "It's over, Trent. Mrs. Parks is right."

Trent scowled and turned away. "I won't go! You can't make me."

Don approached him. "We shouldn't have to, Trent. Think of Trixie. This is what's best for her and for you and Bridget. For all of you together."

The boy remained turned away, but the rigidity in his shoulders softened.

"Okay," Don said. "Rick's driving the van. It holds eight, right?" Rick nodded. "Good," Don continued, pointing to each as he spoke their name. "Riding with him will be Les, Uncle Miltie, Trixie, Bridget, Estelle, Barb and Marge. That leaves Gracie, Paul, Trent, Rocky and me."

"In my car?" Rocky's eyes flew open. "No way."

Don pursed his lips. "Okay, how about this? *I'll* go with Rick, and Trixie will come with you guys." He glanced at the little girl. "Hey, Trix. Ready to go with Mrs. Parks?"

Trixie blinked. She looked like she was about to cry.

"She'll go with her sister," Gracie said.

Bridget nodded.

"Trent can still go with you then," Rick said. "That will allow you more help in digging out Rocky's car."

Don clapped his hands. "Great! Everybody get dressed. This troop's moving out!"

The journey back to the road was almost enjoyable. The wind had died, and though the temperature was in the teens, the sun shone, brilliantly glancing off the hardened snow. With Trixie and Uncle Miltie cheering them on, the three men easily hauled the sled, yanking it over the crust, out toward the highway and the waiting van.

Barb started humming *Joy to the World*. The others immediately jumped in, and soon the entire bunch belted out all the verses. After the first run-through, they stopped, laughing and hugging one another, oblivious to the cold. As they reached Rick's van, their voices echoed crisply over the wind-hardened winterland. Barb clapped her hands and congratulated them.

To everyone's relief, the van started immediately. Rick handed Don an extra shovel, then tooted the horn, signaling that he would wait for them.

As Rocky reached his own car, however, he groaned. The snow plow had pushed a wall of ice against the tiny black sedan.

He handed Gracie the keys. While she warmed up the vehicle, Rocky grabbed his own emergency spade and joined Paul in digging.

For the next twenty minutes, they alternated, chipping and digging, until the rest of the little car emerged. With Gracie at the wheel, and the men positioned to push, she gently pressed the accelerator. The car rocked forward, tires whining, then slipped back. Gracie stiffened at the sharp pains suddenly shooting in her neck and breathed deeply, trying to relax.

The men heaved the sedan, back and forth, three times, until the tires finally caught, throwing a trail of snow in their tracks. With a final collective grunt, the car popped free, and Gracie brought it under control and then to a halt.

Once all the passengers were buckled in, she turned to Rocky, with a rare chance to make good use of one of her mother's favorite phrases, "Home, James. And don't spare the horses."

26

I'M SURE I DON'T KNOW what you mean by *abandoning* my nieces and nephew," Harriet Kimball said, her voice rising defensively. "I've done *no* such thing." She paused for a breath.

The receiver to her ear, Gracie headed to the kettle. She glanced out the kitchen window. With the Monday sun rising behind them, Uncle Miltie and Trent stood in the middle of the driveway, their shadows sharply defined against the drifts of snow sweeping across her front lawn. Trent was leaning on his shovel, head thrown back in laughter. Ruddy face beaming, her uncle seemed to be demonstrating something. One hand on his walker, the other moved quickly through the chilly air, as though conducting an orchestra.

"They're doing just fine," Harriet was saying. "I speak to them regularly. And anyway, Bridget's old enough to be in charge of them. She keeps telling me that I needn't hurry back. I was *fourteen*, you know, when I took over the raising of my sisters."

"And would you say that was the best thing for all of you?"

Another pause. "We did all right."

"I'm sure you did," Gracie replied quickly. "However, things are different now."

Harriet Kimball drew a breath, then spoke again, her tone softer. "How are they? Guess little Trixie's looking forward to Christmas?"

"She's very excited, yes."

There was a distant noise, and Gracie could hear another woman's voice. "I wouldn't have left without good reason, Mrs. Parks. My sister's . . . uh . . . well, she's got cancer. And, George—that's my brother-in-law—he's hopeless. He just won't accept it. I didn't plan on being gone this long. But I can't leave her now."

The anger and righteousness that had sharpened Gracie's voice at the beginning of their conversation evaporated like the steam now curling from the kettle. She felt ashamed, then scolded herself, recalling the quote from Plato: *Be kind, for everyone you meet is fighting a hard battle.* The woman's doing her best. Under particularly trying circumstances and what do you do? Judge her before you know all the facts. Nothing's ever black and white, Gracie. You know that. So, where are your Christian ideals of support and forgiveness?

"Look, Mrs. Kimball, I'm—"

"Sorry, Mrs. Parks!" she said in a rush. "Got to go. Give my love to the kids. I'll call you when I can."

The line went dead.

Gracie hung her head and silently prayed.

"You okay?" Uncle Miltie asked.

Her head snapped up in surprise. Rubbing her neck, she replied, "Fine."

Her uncle reached into the freezer, grabbed a bag of peas and handed it to her. "Try this." He then took the beeping receiver out of her hand and returned it to the cradle.

"No, really, I'm all right."

Ignoring her, Uncle Miltie gently draped the bag across her neck and held it in place.

Gracie moaned at the sting of the cold, but it quickly dulled the pain. "Thanks." She patted his hand and held the bag of vegetables to her neck herself. "That does feel better."

"You're always taking care of everyone else, dear. Somebody's got to be on the lookout for you."

She smiled at him. Oh, she was blessed! "I'm grateful."

"And so am I," he replied. He grinned back. "Now, is that a fresh pot of tea?"

In no time, he had poured two mugs of tea and added milk. Handing one to his niece, he sat across from her. "So," he said, taking a sip. "Who were you talking to?"

Gracie answered, "Harriet Kimball."

Her uncle's blue eyes narrowed. "The children's aunt?" He snorted. "She's got some nerve, that one. Leaving those kids on their own." A slight smile touched his lips as he wiped off a drop. "I suppose you straightened her out?"

"That's just it," Gracie replied. "I was on my high-horse to do just that but . . ." Gooseberry jumped onto her lap. He gently kneaded her sweatpants for a moment, then curled into the crook of her arm. She removed the cold compress and stroked him under the chin.

His fur was cold, his paws slightly damp. Funny how he always knew when she was troubled.

"You know, Uncle Miltie? She's not a bad person, at all. She's got her own troubles, you see. A dying sister, a devastated brother-in-law . . . from the sounds of it, she's always had to be the responsible one. Of course, she shouldn't have left those kids unattended but . . . in her own mind, she didn't do anything any different from what had been her own experience."

"You never know, do you?" He set his mug down carefully. "Guess the kids complicated matters."

"Bridget reassured her that they were fine, that she needn't hurry back on their account." She looked across at her uncle. "I keep asking myself: What would I have done in the same situation?"

Uncle Miltie banged the table. Gooseberry's head popped

up, huge green eyes watchful. "You'd have called in the authorities. Gotten some help."

"Even if it meant that the children might be split up?"

"You don't know that's what Harriet Kimball was thinking, do you?" He poured more tea into both mugs.

"No, but that's what I'd be thinking."

"Aunt Harriet!"

Gracie looked up. Trent Freeman stood in the kitchen doorway, obviously upset by what he'd heard.

"She's not coming back, is she?" he demanded. "You promised, Mrs. Parks!" At the sound of his angry voice, Gooseberry leapt off Gracie's lap and skittered across the slippery kitchen. Sliding to a back-arched stop, he then bolted out of the room. "You promised!"

"Now, just one minute, young man!" Uncle Miltie was stern.

Gracie quickly rose to her feet. "You're a guest in our house, Trent Freeman," she said sternly. "And, as such, you'll behave with proper courtesy."

Trent scowled. "But, Mrs. Parks," he began. "You know what—"

"If you have a problem," Gracie interrupted. "Then, by all means, let's discuss it. But don't think shouting in my kitchen is going to do anything but disappoint us and stretch your vocal cords."

"Sorry," the boy mumbled.

"That's not how your mother taught you to apologize, is it?" Uncle Miltie asked.

Trent flushed. "No, sir." He took a deep breath, then looked directly at Gracie. "I'm sorry, ma'am. I really am. It's just that—"

Uncle Miltie frowned.

"Forget it. I'm sorry," Trent said. "Please."

"Apology accepted," Gracie said. "Now, come sit down and have some breakfast."

Trent did as he was told. As he devoured a huge bowl of cereal, Gracie scrambled a couple of eggs and fried a few strips of bacon while briefly telling him an abridged version of her conversation with his aunt. Uncle Miltie cut the brown bread and slathered two slices with butter.

"So, she's not coming back?"

She spooned the food onto his plate. Uncle Miltie brought over a pot of strawberry jam. "Her sister—your other aunt— isn't very well. Your Aunt Harriet just isn't sure when she'll be free to come back to Willow Bend."

The boy shivered. "Never, I hope. She always made us feel like we'd done something wrong, even when we hadn't. Honest! She doesn't even like to cook, at least not for us." He forked in another mouthful. "*Mmm* . . . this is good, Mrs. Parks. I kind of failed at cooking myself breakfasts like this." He shrugged. "I tried scrambling eggs a couple of times, but

I kept biting into egg shells. Ugh." He stuck out his tongue.

"What do you mean, *you* made the eggs?" Uncle Miltie asked.

"Well, that was after Aunt Harriet. She'd get us up real early. Before sunrise. The girls would have to clean something, like wash the kitchen floor or scrub the bathroom walls, and I'd be sent outside to chop more wood." He shook his head. "I bet you I chopped enough wood to heat all of Willow Bend."

Gracie remembered Don's comment about the size of the wood pile at the Freemans.

He spread Gracie's homemade jam on his bread and took a large bite. "Bridget's as bad a cook as me so we had cereal. Every day. Sometimes with water when we'd forgotten to buy milk." He chewed a last bit of bread, staring at Gracie. "You're going to help us, aren't you? Tell them that we're doing okay? I mean, you're not going to let them split us up or anything, right?"

Gracie examined his earnest young face and sighed. If only it were that easy. "I can't promise that, Trent."

"But what are—"

"Hold on a minute!" Uncle Miltie interrupted. "Let her finish."

Biting his lip, Trent waited.

Gracie spoke confidently. She didn't know how she was going to do it. But she did know she'd have help. From her uncle, her friends, and of course, from Him. She silently recalled a quote from Robert Schuller—*Faith is making commitments before you can be assured that everything will work out*—then offered up a prayer for guidance.

"What I can and do promise you is that I'll do everything in my power to make sure that you and your sisters remain together. Okay?"

Trent released his lip along with a drawn-out sigh. "Okay. I trust you, Mrs. Parks. You've been fair with me."

"What's wrong?"

He flushed, hair falling over his face. "You're going to laugh. Both of you."

Gracie and her uncle exchanged a glance. "Try us," Uncle Miltie said.

The boy swallowed. "Well, my mom, she . . . uh . . . she really believed in God, you know? And . . . and I try to, because that would mean she's safe, up there in heaven. Right?"

They nodded encouragingly.

"She said that we all have . . . *don't laugh* . . . guardian angels. Someone who watches over us." He smiled so sweetly that Gracie fought back tears. "Told us that she was our guardian angel and that she'd always look out for us. No matter what."

He pushed the hair from his eyes. Uncle Miltie blinked and reached for a tissue.

"Since she . . . well, you know . . . I haven't felt like she was with me. Until I met you, Mrs. Parks."

This time, Gracie's tears flowed freely. Uncle Miltie grabbed her hand and squeezed.

"You care." Trent dropped his eyes. "I think my mom's asked God to let you be my guardian angel." His hazel eyes suddenly locked onto hers. "I'm so glad."

LATER THAT MORNING, Gracie went straight to work. It took three phone calls until she finally reached the right office, the one whose mandate, the voice on the answering machine coolly informed her, was to serve Indiana children who are at risk of abuse or neglect. Although she preferred not to reveal her identity, Gracie knew that getting the right information was essential. She left her name and number but was no further than she'd been when she started.

Then she remembered Rocky saying that the *Gazette* had previously published a piece on children in care. She quickly called the paper.

"Well, hello, Gracie!" the editor's deep voice filled her ear. "You thawed out? That was some adventure, wasn't it? Everything all right with the kids?"

She assured him that it was. "I'm doing some research on social services. You mentioned that Sue Jameson did a related feature?"

"Yup. A few months back. Want a copy?"

Gracie pondered for a moment. "Well, really, I'm just looking for the name of a local contact."

"Makes sense. I'll ask her. . . . Hang on a sec, she's walking by. I'm lucky she got here today! Sue!"

"Still there?" he asked, returning in a minute.

"Yes."

"Got a pen? Sue's contact was Emily Wicks, she's a Family Services social worker."

"Emily Wicks?" Gracie asked. "You sure?"

"Yeah. Why?"

Gracie frowned. "It's somehow familiar . . . I know her, or something about her. I just can't remember what it is."

"It wouldn't surprise me if you knew her, that's for sure. You know everyone. Try thinking of something funny. That's what I do."

"Does it work?"

She could almost hear his smile. "No, but it makes me laugh." He gave her the phone number, then mentioned that he was considering writing a feature on their icy escapade. "Game to be interviewed? I'm sure there are a lot of folks who'd like your recipe for burnt-kernel granola."

"Very funny. Thanks for the help." She hung up and stared at the name she had just written down. "Emily Wicks," she said aloud. "Emily Wicks. Now where in the world have I heard that before?"

Baffled, she started the dishes. She kept running the name

around in her head. Finally, becoming frustrated, she stared outside onto the glistening sheet of snow and noticed her rhododendron bushes peeking above the partially buried post-and-rail fence. Looking at her garden brought to mind her uncle's latest groaner. *LITTLE SISTER: I'm going outside to water the flowers. OLDER SISTER: But it's raining! LITTLE SISTER: That's okay. I'll wear my raincoat.*

She chuckled despite herself. That's when it hit her: Emily Wicks was Pat Allen's sister! Though Emily wasn't a regular congregation member, she did come to the second Sunday service on occasion. Gracie had also met her at the occasional church function. She silently saluted Rocky's memory technique and punched the number for the church's office.

"Season's greetings! Eternal Hope Community Church. Pat Allen speaking."

"Oh, Pat! It's Gracie. I'm so glad you're in. Blessings of the season to you, too."

"Gracie! How nice to hear from you. Paul is getting a lot of mileage out of the choir's arctic adventures. Is everyone really all right?"

"Just fine. Still a little chilled, maybe, but otherwise fine. We've all got a lot to be thankful for."

"Yes." Pat's voice dropped. "Don't know if you're aware of it, but when Paul discovered you were all missing, he gathered friends for an impromptu prayer service."

For a moment, Gracie couldn't speak. Finally, she managed,

"Blessings, Pat. How grateful I am. I'm glad you told me. You're both such good friends. I'll thank Paul in person next time I see him."

"Oh, no," Pat told her. "He doesn't want you to know how concerned he really was—now that you're safe and sound, it's enough that the prayers were answered. But now, what is it I can do for you?"

Gracie hesitated. "I need to ask you something, but I can't really tell you why. Will you just trust me that it's *very* important and that I'll tell you everything when I'm able?"

Anyone else would have been consumed with curiosity but, without hesitation, the practical woman replied, "Of course, Gracie. How can I help?"

"Where does your sister Emily work?"

"She's a county social worker. For a least twenty years now."

"I urgently need to speak with her. May I ask you for her work number?"

"No problem." It was Pat's turn to hesitate. "I don't mean to be stepping in where I don't belong but . . . would it help if I called her right now and asked her to phone you immediately?"

"Oh, Pat, would you? Thank you! That would be wonderful."

Gracie hung up the phone. With the pageant less than a week away, and Christmas following shortly after, there were a million things she should be doing. But she couldn't concentrate on them while her mind was occupied with how she was going to fulfill her promise to Trent.

She prayed silently while pacing from the kitchen to the living room and back. From his perch on the chair near the living room window, Gooseberry's green eyes followed her, the tip of his tail twitching. *Lord, You've put me in this position of trust. Now, what do I do? The lives of three orphan children are in my hands. I know You have a plan—I can feel that You're guiding me—and that You'd never forsake me, but if it wouldn't be too much trouble, could You let me in on it as soon as possible?* She stopped and stroked her cat for a long time. *Until then, I guess I'll just keep going, hoping and praying You'll keep me headed in the right direction.*

The phone interrupted her thoughts. It was Emily Wicks.

"Hello, Emily," Gracie replied, trying to keep the nervousness out of her voice. "Thank you for calling me so quickly. I realize we've barely spoken but—"

"Nonsense," Emily interrupted. "My sister's told me so much about you, I feel as if I know you. I've heard your choir sing many times. Now," she continued, with the same efficient manner as her sister, "as you know, Pat's not prone to exaggeration, so when she said you urgently needed my help, I knew I had to call right away. I don't mean to rush you, but I've a busy schedule so if you don't mind, let's get straight to it. What's the problem?"

Taking a moment to collect herself, Gracie then related to her all the necessary facts.

"*Hmm*," Emily replied. "Let me recap: three orphaned kids. Oldest is seventeen, youngest is eight. No suitable family members available to take care of them. Is that right?"

Imagining the other woman writing everything down in a precise, clear hand, Gracie replied yes.

"Pretty familiar scenario. The state's policy is to place the children—that's anyone under eighteen—in the least restrictive, most familylike setting that meets their needs. That's tough, though not impossible, without immediate family available. First things, first. We have twenty-four-hour foster care for children who are no longer safe in their homes, due to abuse or neglect or other unsatisfactory behaviors. Your kids would certainly qualify."

Gracie asked the question she feared the most. "Would they be split up?"

There was a long silence. "That's another tough one, Gracie. You see, we do our best to keep families together, but the reality often ends up being very different. There aren't too many foster homes that would be able to accommodate three children, especially given their ages. I'd have to have to know a lot more."

Though she was expecting that information, Gracie still felt a wave of panic. Suddenly, a new question popped unbidden into her mind and her panic vanished. "What sort of living arrangements are acceptable?"

"*Hmm.* There are a few, but as I mentioned earlier, the best solution is to place the children with an approved relative. Lacking that, you've got the possibility of a licensed foster family home—as I said, this would be tough given your *hypothetical* scenario—a group home, a child-caring institution or another court-approved facility."

A glimmer of hope appeared on the horizon. "What's 'another court-approved facility'?"

"That's really a catch-all phrase to accommodate more, shall we say, creative solutions. It could be any number of scenarios, as long as the state's satisfied that the children's best interests are at heart. Again, I'd have to know all the circumstances. Why? You've got something in mind for your kids?"

Gracie answered, "I'm not sure."

Emily was still brisk. "If you want further information and are able to provide me with more details, I'd be happy to meet with you. In the meantime, I'll forget that we had this conversation, though I have to say I think you have posed a problem I should be taking an interest in."

Gracie agreed and thanked her. *So,* she thought, after replacing the receiver, *You* are *directing me. There is something You want me to realize . . . some solution . . . I just know it.* She shook her head. *I'm trying to see it, dear Lord, but I just can't.*

Not yet, anyway. She sighed and looked around. Usually she felt that the best place to solve a problem was alone with God in the warmth of her kitchen. She sighed again. Not today. Today, she needed air, a chance to get her muscles and brain cells firing.

Of course! She grinned to herself and with renewed energy, dressed for the wintry air. After all, the second best place to solve a problem was alone with God on a long morning walk, even if slippery patches of snow and ice proved distracting.

28

AS GRACIE STRODE OUT, Willow Bend still looked just about picture perfect! In a scene straight from a Christmas card, soft rolls of glistening snow carpeted the lawns and streets, and icicles highlighted the trees' latticework of branches. Confident in her sturdy, thick-soled boots, Gracie charged along for several blocks, nimbly avoiding slippery patches and icy chunks of snow. Though her mind still reeled with questions and worries about her new responsibilities, she was invigorated as she marched happily downtown.

Approaching Barry's Barber Shop, she stopped to admire the tiny twinkling Christmas tree decorated with miniature combs and brushes. Despite her thick hat and scarf, Barry recognized her through the window and cheerfully waved his straight razor. A man, his face half-shaved, grinned at her from the barber's chair. It took her a moment to identify him as Mayor Tom Ritter. Smiling broadly, she tapped the window three times in salute, then moved quickly on.

Behind the stained-glass clock at Main and Cherry, which honored Willow Bend's war dead, stood a huge Christmas tree, alive with sparkling tinsel, spinning ornaments, and glowing red lights. A small knot of families was gathered in front of The Sweet Shoppe. She recognized young Patsy Clayton, bundled up in her wheelchair, accompanied by her mother. Gracie nodded to Marilyn Clayton, then bent over to give Patsy a hug. The little girl, who lived next door to Amy Cantrell, was a courageous fighter, never diminished in spirit, no matter how much her body suffered.

"It's lovely to see you again, Gracie," Marilyn said, taking control of the wheelchair. "Did you know Patsy has a part in the pageant?"

"I'm a *narrator*," Patsy interrupted proudly.

Marilyn continued, "I promised her some sort of turban headdress, and now, we're out looking to find something that will fill the bill."

"Come see me!" Patsy commanded Gracie. "And bring Gooseberry, too. I'll bet the manger could use a cat!"

As Gracie continued along Main Street, her thoughts turned inward, away from the cheery decorations she was passing, and to the quiet, fundamental truth young Patsy represented: Hope is everything.

If crippled Patsy's vision encompassed hope and healing, then surely Gracie Parks should follow her lead. It had to be easier to keep one small family together than the more stubborn matter of a crippled body.

Then she stepped into the warmth of the offices of the *Mason County Gazette*.

"Stop right there!" Rocky Gravino ordered, rising from behind his large desk. Gracie froze, rivulets of snow dribbling down her shoulders. "I know just what you need. Come on," he added, shrugging into his heavy parka and flinging a tartan scarf around his neck. He shouted good-bye to his staff.

Without another word, he took Gracie by the arm and marched her outside. After half a block, he turned and stopped.

Gracie blinked in surprise. They were facing the window of The Sweet Shoppe!

"Stow that," Rocky ordered, hustling her inside. "Nothing like a hot fudge sundae to brighten one's spirits."

"But . . . ." she started again.

"Two hot fudge sundaes, please," Rocky ordered. "Extra fudge on both." He spied an open booth near the back. Pointing, he said, "Grab that one, Gracie. I'll be there in a jiffy."

Amazed at the number of people eating ice cream in the

dead of winter, Gracie wandered to the back in a daze. Hadn't she been out for an invigorating prayer-walk?

"There!" Rocky said, plunking two large glass containers onto the table. Rivers of fudge streamed down the rounded balls of vanilla ice cream. A cherry was poised atop each. He handed her a long-handled spoon and, still in his parka, dove right in. "Eat. We'll talk later."

She did as she was told. After the first bite, when the rush of ice cream slid down her throat, she sighed and happily consumed the rest. Finally, when she wiped her lips and leaned back, he smiled.

"I didn't even know I was hungry."

"Ha!" He slowly licked a puddle of chocolate off his spoon. "Hunger's got nothing to do with dessert. You know that. The body needs sugar, Gracie, my girl. From the look on your face when you stumbled into my office, I knew I had to act quickly."

"Stumbled?"

Rocky nodded. "Your expression was a fascinating combination of . . ." he paused. "Well, of hope and despair. That's it! Layered together like a sandwich cookie." He stretched across to pat her arm. "Care to talk about it? I'm a good listener. I just hope it's two parts hope to one of despair!"

Gracie shifted on the hard bench.

"It's about the Freeman kids. Right?"

Nodding, she said, "I've spoken to Emily Wicks, Sue's contact."

"And," he gently prodded.

"I'm afraid it's not good news. We didn't get into specific details but . . ." she pushed her spoon. "I think it'll be difficult to find a foster home for all three of them."

Neither spoke for a couple of minutes. The bell above the door jangled and the drawer of the cash register banged with the ebb and flow of hardy ice cream addicts.

"The girl, Bridget, isn't old enough, I suppose?" Rocky asked.

"No. Eighteen's the minimum age and even then, it's a lot of responsibility for a young woman."

"There must be a way, Gracie. The girl's almost eighteen." He glanced down, suddenly realizing that he was still dressed for outdoors. Blushing slightly, he tugged off his coat and hat. The papers slid from his pocket.

"What's that?"

He held them. "Draft of my article on Florence Jackson. Thought you might give it a glance before it goes to print. Of course, under the circumstances, don't worry. I'll ask Sue."

She touched his hand, so large compared with her own. It was warm. "No. I'd love to read it. May I?"

As she read it, she realized she liked best a particularly lyrical quote: "'I adore the alchemy of clay,' the raven-haired potter declared. 'The way it mingles fire, water, air and the earth. It's so alive! This may sound funny but it reminds me of fly-fishing. Feet on the ground, water rushing by, a neatly balanced rod in my hands and the graceful curve of the wire when a fish leaps into the air to take the bait.'"

But Gracie also was affected by the last paragraph. "'If only my dear Lew were still alive. He was my inspiration. I'm so lost without him.'"

Gracie swallowed, unable to speak. Memories of Elmo flooded over her. She softly said, "That's lovely, Rocky. Absolutely lovely. I wouldn't change a word."

"I'm very pleased you like it. After all, it was your idea." He took in her joy-struck expression. "Come on, give! What *are* you thinking?"

A remarkable idea had flown into her mind. Angellike, one might almost say. "Do me a favor? Don't print that story just yet." She was not only joyful but excited.

"Huh? I thought you said it was good?"

"It is. I just think I might have a happier ending for it."

GRACIE BENT HER HEAD against the wind and turned for home. Just then, her cell phone rang. "Hello?" she gasped.

"Gracie?"

Recognizing the voice of the chief of police, she shoved the instrument under her scarf and hat. "Herb? Yes, it's me. What can I do for you?"

"Sorry to trouble you, but is Trent Freeman staying with you?"

Thoughts racing, Gracie almost bit her tongue. How did he find out? Did he know about the girls? What would he do if she told him the truth? "Well," she began, uncertain what to say.

"Don't worry. I'm asking as a peace officer, not as a social worker. Look, Estelle told Marybeth everything. How you folks got stranded at the Freeman house and brought the kids into town. From what Estelle said, you're trying to work out their situation."

Gracie breathed more evenly and began marching to keep warm as Herb continued, "I don't see any reason for my involvement. At least, not now. What I do need is a chance to speak with Trent."

She heard him sigh deeply.

"The heat's on in more than one way, if you catch my drift, to find my mother-in-law's bracelet. It's not worth much but . . . as far as we know, nobody's tried to fence it—which would have happened if some petty thief had been needing fast cash—so I'm still looking for an answer."

"Why Trent?"

"His sister happened to mention that he was shoveling snow in front of the senior center the afternoon the bracelet was declared missing."

Gracie stopped short. "You don't suspect Trent!"

"No, but as a matter of course he's got to be questioned. He might have seen or heard something. Thing is, I'd been leaving messages for his aunt, but she never returned my calls. Of course, now I know why. So, is he staying with you?"

Gracie replied, "Yes. And his sisters are next door with Marge." She tugged up her glove and checked her watch. "Can you meet me at my place in, say, fifteen minutes?"

"Righto."

Herb Bower's cruiser was already in her driveway as Gracie came around the corner and rushed up her walk. Slipping into the kitchen door, she was immediately assailed by a din of excited voices. Before she had removed her boots, Trixie flew into her arms. Hat in hand, Herb loomed in the living room entrance. Marge and Bridget perched in kitchen chairs, as though ready to flee. Near the sink, stood Trent and her uncle, one arm protectively around the boy's shoulders.

They all spoke to her at once. Gracie raised her right hand, signaling silence. After a moment, the voices slowly died. "Right," she said.

"He's going to take us away!" Bridget said in a low, sad voice.

"No!" Gracie was firm. "Listen to me! Chief Bower's not here to take you away or to break you up. Okay? He just wants to talk to Trent about the day Mrs. Simmons's bracelet disappeared."

Trent's eyes darted toward his sister.

"Look, son, I'll ask Mrs. Parks to join us, so we can talk, just the three of us, for a couple of minutes?"

Gracie squeezed Trent's hand and smiled as they followed the burly policeman into the living room. Herb appropriated the big armchair near the window while Gracie and Trent settled themselves on the couch.

"Okay, Trent," Herb started, his voice kind. "This shouldn't take long. I understand you were shoveling snow in front of the building on the afternoon Mrs. Simmons's bracelet disappeared."

Trent looked wary. "Yeah. Later on."

"Did you see anything unusual?"

"Like what?" Trent was cautious.

Herb chuckled softly. "Did you see anyone acting suspiciously? For example, leaving in a hurry, or looking out of place. That sort of thing."

Trent shrugged. "A few people came and went. I didn't pay any attention. I didn't really go inside. They've got a wide walkway and that Mrs. Cook kept coming out and telling me to make sure I'd cleaned it, right down to the pavement."

"Well," Herb said, putting his hands on his knees. "Thanks. That's all." He handed the boy a business card. "If you think of anything, give me a call, okay?" The police chief rose. "Well, thanks, Gracie. I'll be off."

"Sure you can't stay for coffee?"

"Thanks, but I'd better get going."

She walked him to the front door. Trent hovered near the entrance to the kitchen, watching the policeman. As Herb zipped up his quilted parka, her uncle suddenly appeared and, seeing Herb, stopped to exchange greetings.

"Sorry again about your angels, Uncle Miltie," Herb said. "Bad enough at the center but in the church!" He shook his head. "Nasty business."

Uncle Miltie nodded. "Hope you find the scoundrel."

Herb sighed. "Me, too. Well, thanks again. See you."

"Bye, Herb! Give our love to Marybeth!" Marge shouted from the kitchen.

When Gracie returned, Bridget and Marge were finishing the dishes while Trixie was looking at a book at the kitchen table. "I'm just going to make a short phone call, Marge," Gracie said. "Can you wait for a few minutes before you and the girls head home for supper?"

Her friend nodded.

Trent lightly grabbed her arm as she moved into the living room. "What did the broken angels in the church have to do with Uncle Miltie?"

Thoughts already on her next conversation, Gracie replied while picking up the receiver, "He made them. Now, if you'll excuse me for a minute . . ."

"Oh, uh, sure." He disappeared up the stairs.

The call she placed was brief. It was one she didn't want the others to hear. After a quick but incomplete explanation, she asked, "Could you drop by tomorrow afternoon? About four?"

The voice said yes.

Just as Gracie replaced the receiver, the phone rang.

"Hello?"

"Oh, hi, Gracie! It's Linda."

"Hello. How's everyone?" Gracie replied, delighted to hear from the mother of her choir's star soprano.

"We're all fine, thanks. Amy's been telling me about your ordeal. *Brrrr!*"

"We had our fellowship to keep us warm," Gracie replied, meaning it.

"You all were certainly courageous!"

"Necessity is the mother of invention . . . and of that kind of courage. But what can I do for you?"

"Well, it's the other way around, really. I know the Freeman kids are staying with you and Marge. Oh, Gracie!" her voice suddenly pitched higher. "I can't *tell* you how bad I felt when I heard about their aunt leaving them! So dreadfully irresponsible!"

She took a breath. "Anyway, I've been speaking to Tish and Tyne and we'd all like to help, including our husbands. Bridget's in several of Amy's classes, and when I think of my own daughter being left to fend for herself and two siblings, well, I just can't imagine! So, what can we do? Drive them to school or sports events? Do they need any clothes? Just tell me what you need. Between us, we should be able to make it easier on you."

Although Gracie was concerned that the whereabouts of the Freeman children was becoming common knowledge, she was touched by Linda's generously extended offer. "Well, we have been overwhelmed a bit ever since we got home. I just haven't had a chance to think. May I talk it over with Marge and get back to you? Believe me, I'm appreciative—I just am not certain what's the best help you can give."

"I don't want to pressure you, of course. Take your time but remember, we're available."

Gracie thanked her again and hung up.

"Who was that?" Marge asked, entering the living room.

Before Gracie had time to reply, the phone jangled again. It was Abe Wasserman.

"Hey, Gracie! Look, I'm taking a break from the grill, so I'll be quick. Amy was telling me about your unexpected house guests. Poor kids! Being left alone! It breaks your heart." Gracie tried to speak, but Abe kept rolling. "Anyway, I know you're busy so I'll come to the point. I wanted to warn you that Amy'll be dropping by on her way home. I've baked a tray of honey cookies that I want you and Marge to have."

Gracie was so taken aback, she couldn't find her breath.

"I must go! You take care now!"

"Thank you, dear Abe," she told him. Tears filled her eyes. "Thank you," she repeated to the dial tone.

"What's wrong?" Marge leaned forward with concern.

Gracie sniffled and grabbed her friend's hands. "Nothing. It . . . it's just that our friends are so generous!" She quickly told Marge what had happened.

"Well, I'll be," Marge replied, reaching for a tissue. "Isn't that a blessing?"

AN HOUR LATER, the doorbell rang. With Uncle Miltie napping and Trent upstairs reading, Gracie was alone in the kitchen. She dropped the vegetable peeler and went to the front door. Amy Cantrell stood on the stoop. Refusing Gracie's invitation to come in, she explained that she was late for her own supper and handed her a pastry box.

"Enjoy the treats! I didn't touch them. Promise!" She turned to go. "Oh, hello, Goosie!" she cried, reaching down as the large orange tomcat streaked past her legs into the cool darkness. Grinning, she looked back at Gracie. "That cat's getting crazier by the minute!" She skipped down the porch steps. "Well, see you at the pageant!"

Gracie put down the box and waved at Amy's retreating car. Turning to close the door, she spied Gooseberry gingerly picking his way across the snow. Knowing how much he hated to get his paws wet, Gracie stared in astonishment. Pausing for a moment, Gooseberry sniffed, then with a twist, dashed through a catflap into the garage. Another movement caught her eye. As she looked around, Gracie noticed a light coming from the garage window.

Wasn't her uncle napping still? She headed for his small workspace.

"Who's there?" she called, as she opened the door. "Uncle Miltie?" Why was it dark?

There was a muffled thump, then Gooseberry dropped from the workbench.

A thin white face stared at her, blinded. A pair of hands flew up to block the light. Her cat hissed, then stalked out.

"Trent!" she cried out in shock and relief. "Good heavens! You gave me a start." She walked in. "What are you doing here, in the dark?"

Still shading his eyes, Trent mumbled, "Uh . . . looking for a scraper. The car windows will need it tomorrow." He paused. She heard more rustling. "Oh!" he suddenly said, his tone exaggerated. "Forgot what time it is. Gotta go!"

"Hey!" she shouted at his back. "Wait a minute . . ." For a moment, she stood there. Obviously, he was lying, and this troubled her. He was, after all, living under her roof. Then she remembered her son, Arlen, at about Trent's age. How, when he'd been in some sort of trouble, he often needed a little time. Just enough for his conscience to compel him into telling the truth.

She knew that Trent Freeman was a decent young man. His devotion to his sisters was admirable. And he obviously wanted to please Gracie and Uncle Miltie—only, for him, as with all teenagers, pleasing adults worked best when it also suited him to do so.

"AHA!" UNCLE MILTIE CRIED the next afternoon, laying a playing card onto the kitchen table with a flourish. "See, Trix?" he said, glancing at the little girl who sat beside him. "I win. Again."

Trixie giggled and reached into her lap to stroke Gooseberry's chin. Eyes closed, purring loudly, the big cat spilled across her narrow lap, legs dangling.

Her brother tossed his cards on the table in frustration. Gracie was at the sink, peeling potatoes, and watching with amusement. Trent hadn't mentioned last night.

"That's the third straight game, Uncle Miltie," the boy said. "You got another deck up your sleeve?"

Uncle Miltie raised his eyebrows in mock surprise. "When you've played Hearts as long as I have, young man, you don't need to cheat."

"I was only kidding," Trent replied hastily. Gracie shot him a look. He flushed slightly and turned away.

"Of course you were. Hand over one of those chocolate cookies and all's forgiven."

Trent grinned and dug into the cookie jar.

The doorbell rang.

Leaping to his feet, Trent shouted, "I'll get it!"

He returned in a minute with Florence Jackson. Wearing a scarlet cloak and matching tam, the potter swooped into the kitchen.

"Flo!" Uncle Miltie and Gracie cried out together.

"Hello, you two." She approached Uncle Miltie and laid her hands gently on his shoulders. "I'm so glad you're safe and sound." She leaned over to squeeze Gracie's hand, then gave her a quick wink. "And who else have we here?" she asked, turning to the children. "I've already met the handsome Master Trent. And Bridget I also know from the center."

"I'm Trixie," the little girl shouted, tugging at Flo's cloak.

Flo bent to one knee and hugged Trixie. "Of course, you are, darling." She turned. "Trent? Would you mind bringing in my boxes? Careful, though. The contents are extremely fragile."

Uncle Miltie took her cloak and hat as the rest settled back into kitchen chairs. Gracie asked, "Would you like coffee?"

"Tea, please," Flo replied.

Trent returned and carefully laid a large box in front of her. Another trip produced two smaller boxes. Reaching into one of them, Flo pulled out a pair of lambs trailing foam bits, and declared, "Hope you like these. Uncle Miltie worked very hard to get them finished."

Trixie asked politely, her eyes aglow, "May I touch one?"

"Of course, dear," Flo replied, sliding a kneeling lamb across the table. She took a sip of tea from the mug offered by Gracie. "Just remember, be gentle."

As the girl ran her fingers over the hard white surface, Flo dug into another box, this time removing a much larger animal.

"A donkey!" Bridget cried, clapping her hands.

"Another Uncle Miltie original!" Flo grinned and passed the braying burro to her. Then, with a quick bow, she reached into the large box.

Even Trent's eyes lit up when the last object came into view. It was the graceful-necked camel that Gracie had earlier seen at the senior center. Painted in a thick caramel color, and highlighted by a ruby-red saddle and matching reins, Gracie could almost hear the single-humped creature sigh as its huge olive eyes stared dreamily into space.

"Oh, Flo!" she cried, rising to give the woman a quick squeeze. "It's magnificent! Any minute, it's going to stroll right off the table." She turned to kiss and hug her uncle. "You, too, you old dear. These are wonderful animals you made! Our church pageant will be very very blessed this year. Thank you, both."

The two artists beamed.

"Where are the rest of your angels, Uncle Miltie?" Flo asked. "We could pack them all up together now."

He hesitated. "No, we can't. They're all broken."

"Are you sure? I thought you'd—"

"Broken," he told her firmly.

Gracie noticed that Trent opened his mouth, as though to speak, then didn't.

"You made the camel?" Bridget questioned Flo. The artist nodded. "Wow. And you made the rest, Uncle Miltie?"

"With Flo's help, yes."

"Wow," she repeated. "Would I ever like to create something like that."

"You can," Flo replied, touching the girl's hand. "I'll teach you."

Bridget looked from Flo to Uncle Miltie. "Really?"

"If she can teach me," Uncle Miltie said. "Anyone can learn."

"Even me?" Trixie asked, her chin resting over the lamb's back.

Flo tweaked her nose. "Especially you." She glanced at Trent, who was looking bored. "How about you?"

He folded his arms across his chest. "No way."

Gracie asked, "Trent, have you noticed Flo's brooch?"

"Brooch?"

"Oh, yes!" Flo said, quickly removing the fish-shaped piece from her lapel. "You might like it." She gave it to the doubtful teenager.

His eyes widened as he examined it. "Is . . . is this what I think it is?" he asked, seeming amazed by what he saw.

"A Turner's Tousled Nymph covered in plastic, yes."

Trent's jaw dropped. "A Turner's Tousl . . ." he repeated automatically. Swallowing, he continued. "Where'd you get this?"

Flo smiled and took one of the cookies offered by Gracie. "Tied it myself."

This last revelation was too much for the boy. He slumped into his chair, shaking his head. "You know how to tie a Turner's Tousled Nymph?"

Flo munched the cookie. She replied, "Un huh . . . a Woolly Shrimpo, a Golden-ribbed Tully. You name a fishing fly, Trent. I can tie it."

This time it was Trent who said "Wow!" Then he peppered her with questions about knots, lines and dubbing, which Flo answered quickly and easily. Faces alive with interest, the girls continued their examinations of the manger animals.

Uncle Miltie leaned across to his niece. "Why do I get the distinct impression," he whispered, "that you aren't as surprised as I am that Flo's here?"

Gracie just smiled.

Her uncle's eyes narrowed. "What have you got up your sleeve, Gracie Parks?"

Her smile only widened. And there was that look of joy again.

THE NEXT AFTERNOON Gracie was scheduled to help set up the manger and so decided to take advantage of her friends' offers to help. She arranged for Trent to visit with fourteen-year-old Jeffrey Larson, while the girls were off to the Cantrells. Marge joined her on the porch as she waved at the Cantrells' van.

"Ready?"

Gracie nodded. Handing a bag of ornaments to Marge, Gracie shouted good-bye to her uncle who was engrossed in an old war movie, then pulled on her coat and boots. They arrived at the church to find that Pastor Paul and a few others had already been busy. In an alcove near the altar lay a couple of boxes. Barb and Estelle were hanging wreaths while Don and Rick carted between them a large rectangular moving crate filled with straw.

"Oh, that smells good," Marge said, grabbing a stalk and giving it a sniff. "Just like my uncle's farm."

Don nodded. "The McIvers brought the hay again this year." He and Rick turned the crate onto its side and began spreading the straw in a semi-circle in front.

Limping slightly, Lester Twomley appeared, carrying a large slab of particle board painted midnight-blue except for a single blazing star whose beams of light streaked down like lightning.

The men propped up the backdrop as Pat Allen and Marge began setting out makeup kits, bits of costumes, beautifully wrapped boxes for the gifts from the Magi and the tiny cot used for the sleeping Christ Child.

"Someone give me a hand?" Paul was at the back entrance.

"Be right there!" Rick answered.

A moment later, they arrived, each carrying a box. Flo Jackson brought up the rear, the last box in her hands.

"Wait until you see these," Gracie said, as they gently laid down their loads.

As Flo removed each animal, the others cheered. Don and Rick carefully placed the lambs near the cot and the donkey in the crate toward the back. Everyone was silent when Flo revealed the camel.

"It's exquisite!" Marge said finally. Pat was beaming. The

others nodded. Pastor Paul took both of Flo's hands into his own as he thanked her. Don gently laid the camel near the front.

"May I speak with you for a minute?" Gracie asked her pastor.

"Sure." He took her arm and led her to a distant pew. "Everything all right with the children?"

Gracie nodded. She briefed him on what she had learned from Emily Wicks.

His brow wrinkled. "Oh dear. So, there's a good chance they'll be split up?"

"Unless we come up with something creative, I'm afraid so. And I mean something creative that will satisfy a social services agency."

He stared at her for a minute. "You've got something in mind. I can see it in your eyes."

Gracie smiled, comforted by the fact that she was revealing her idea in the Lord's house. It just had to be right. "Yes. I wanted to run it by you before I spoke with the authorities. It'll take some explaining and I'm hoping you'll come with me. I've arranged to meet with Emily Wicks tomorrow afternoon."

"Pat's sister?"

She nodded. "She's the one I got the information from."

"I'll be there."

"Well, I think I can convince Emily that the best thing for

these kids is to stay in their own home. That shouldn't be too hard but . . . in order to do so, they'll need an approved foster parent to live with them. Bridget's not quite old enough yet, but she will be soon."

Paul's eyebrows raised slightly. "And that foster parent would be?"

Gracie glanced around and settled on a figure now hanging lights. "Florence Jackson."

He followed her eyes and scratched his head. "Florence Jackson?"

"She's perfect!" She told him how she had already very briefly spoken to her about the idea. "The Freeman farmhouse is large enough for her work and kiln and she'd love taking care of the kids."

Paul cocked his head. "Sounds pretty good, I must admit. Have the children met her?"

The report was positive. "The girls seem keen to learn pottery and Trent likes her because they can talk fly-fishing. Best of all, they stay together as a family," she told him.

"Well, how about that," the young pastor whispered. "Gracie, you're absolutely amazing! How on earth did you think of it?"

She leaned back and gazed at the ceiling. "I didn't."

His eyes followed hers, and they both smiled.

THURSDAY AFTERNOON, Gracie and Pastor Paul were wedged into a tiny cubicle office, staring hopefully at Emily Wicks. Over the social worker's shoulder, the sun had started to set, casting large shadows along the snow-lined street. "You want me to authorize a complete stranger to be the Freeman children's foster parent?" Mrs. Wicks tossed a pen onto her cluttered desktop. "Even before official channels have been gone through?"

A phone rang in an adjoining cubicle, while a young mother and child anxiously waited for an appointment and, nearby, two social workers were involved in a heated exchange over an empty coffee pot.

Gracie ignored the goings-on and concentrated on Emily's face. She had already put forth her case, speaking as clearly and as convincingly as possible. "Well, Don Delano was going to notify Bud Smith, his principal. And Bud was supposed to talk to Helen at the elementary school. But the snow kept everyone at home, and I truly feel the children are best served if we try to solve the problem now.

Paul nodded.

Gracie continued. "Emily, there just isn't much hope of finding an existing foster family to take them in."

With a sigh, the social worker indicated her agreement.

"Given the unacceptable choices of a group home or some sort of institution, I'm certain that letting the Freemans remain in their own home under the care of a loving and responsible adult is exactly in line with your policy of placing children in the least restrictive, most family-like setting."

Emily addressed Paul Meyer. "What do you think, Pastor?" Her eyes were sharp as she awaited his reply.

Without hesitation, he replied, "It's a godsend, Emily. There's no other way to explain it. These three kids were in trouble. The signs were everywhere, from the school absenteeism to their visible exhaustion."

He paused, drawing breath. "We all let them down." He then quickly held up his hands at her defensive expression.

"I mean everyone, not just your organization. In particular, I blame myself. I knew something was wrong but I was too busy with mundane duties to follow my instincts. I kept putting it off, telling myself that their aunt would bring them the next week. I'm sure others had suspicions but . . ." His voice trailed off.

They were silent for a minute, each considering the clergyman's words.

Suddenly, Paul continued with renewed enthusiasm. "Because of what Gracie believes can only be divine intervention, there's a chance to do the right thing. To give both the Freeman children and Mrs. Jackson a better life. Florence is a kind and caring woman who's excited at the prospect of this challenge. I admit I've only spoken to her briefly, but I know she'd cherish living with those kids, and we've seen how they respond to her."

"Won't you at least meet her and the kids?" Gracie asked Emily. "And decide for yourself?"

"Well," Emily replied. "Given that Bridget's approaching legal adulthood, some flexibility may be possible. In the right circumstances."

"Bless you, Emily!" Gracie said. "The pageant's tomorrow night. Trixie's one of the Magi. Why don't you come? They'll all be there. You can see how well they interact with Mrs. Jackson."

"Thank you. You know, you might be right that He's watching over this." Puzzled, they stared at her. Emily Wicks smiled for the first time. "Pat's already invited me."

"There! That's the last of them!" Marge said late Friday morning, pressing the cover on an oversized square cookie tin. She pushed it alongside five matching tins, then leaned onto Gracie's counter and wiped her hands on her apron. The bracelets on her arms tinkled softly, momentarily catching Gooseberry's attention. Willow Bend's finest feline yawned, then returned to his nap atop the refrigerator.

"Okay, what's next?" Marge inquired.

The fondant had melted so Gracie turned off the stove element and removed the pot. "Your timing's perfect. Give me a hand with the last of these mints?"

Using teaspoons, the women dropped the white mixture onto a ribbed rubber mat.

"Think I like the green best," Uncle Miltie said, eyeing the plateful of pastel-colored treats on the kitchen table. He shifted position. "Seasonal. But then so are the red ones. Should I try one of those, just as a bit of quality control?"

Gracie chuckled as her uncle snagged the largest white mint and quickly popped it into his mouth, as though afraid she'd stop him. "Couldn't possibly take them to the church without a proper testing, now could we?"

Once they'd finished dropping the mints, Gracie began washing up while Marge gathered the ingredients for fudge.

"How are the girls doing?" Gracie asked.

"Well, I'm a bit surprised. I thought that I'd be more worried about Trixie fitting in. You know, a little girl away from home in a strange place—but she's doing great! She likes being in the kitchen and helping me cook, and she's excited beyond belief about the pageant! Flo offered to help me sew her costume and between the two of us, we could hardly keep her still."

She paused while cutting a slab of butter. "I'm more concerned about Bridget. I must admit I'm afraid she might have had something to do with Mrs. Simmons's missing bracelet, but she won't discuss it. She's still afraid to trust me with all her secrets, I can tell."

Barely containing his laughter, Uncle Miltie handed her the walnuts. "Don't worry too much, Marge. That's the modus operandi of just about every teenager in America!"

Marge stared at him, then grinned. "Guess you're right." She turned to Gracie. "How's young Trent?"

"He's doing fine, I think. There's something bothering him, too, but . . . he won't talk about it." She shrugged and began peeling the cooled mints off the mat. "Given Uncle Miltie's observation, I guess I shouldn't be surprised."

"They're really sweet kids, you know?" Marge commented. The others nodded. "I'm going to miss them. What do you think will happen to them?" she asked, whipping condensed milk into a bowl of butter. "I'm getting worried."

"Me, too," her uncle added. "None of us wants to see those kids split up. It just isn't right, especially at Christmas."

Gracie slowly handed her friend a bottle of vanilla and a measuring spoon. She had thought of waiting until after the pageant before revealing her plan but didn't feel right about prolonging their pain. "*Umm*, I think I've got good news."

Marge and her uncle both looked at her expectantly.

"Paul and I've spoken with Emily Wicks."

"Pat's sister?" Marge asked.

Gracie nodded. "Yes. She's a social worker. I ran an idea by her, and she thinks it might work."

"What idea?" Uncle Miltie looked ready to mutiny if it was one he didn't approve of.

"Well, not to bore you with the legal details, but without some creative option, the kids likely would be split up. Just as you fear."

Marge looked gloomy.

Uncle Miltie swallowed. "You said, *good* news."

Gracie smiled. "Well, what do you think of Florence Jackson living with the Freemans and acting as their guardian?"

Uncle Miltie's jaw dropped. Marge blinked slowly.

"*My* Florence Jackson?" Uncle Miltie croaked. He swallowed. "So, *that's* why you weren't surprised when she dropped by."

Gracie nodded.

Her uncle's eyes shone with admiration.

Marge found her tongue. "You've spoken to Florence?"

"Yes, but not the kids. Not yet. Flo herself couldn't be more excited. They did seem to get along beautifully. She'll have room for her kiln, maybe even a studio from which she can sell her work. The children will get pampered and protected by a responsible adult. Best of all, they remain together. It's a win-win situation, as Arlen would say."

"Why, that's wonderful!" Marge cried, giving Gracie a big hug. Gooseberry jumped down and bumped against her calves. "And Emily's okay with it?"

Gracie exhaled and tickled the big cat. "Not completely. There's a lot to be considered, but she's agreed to come to the pageant and meet them all. It's a first step."

"It's more than that, my dear," her uncle declared, squeezing her hand. "It's an omen."

34

WITH THE STREETLAMPS and church lights glowing in the starry sky, the Eternal Hope Community Church glittered jewel-like in its winter backdrop. Gracie rolled Fannie Mae into the parking lot while Marge's van pulled alongside.

Everyone tumbled out. Gracie and Marge quickly handed cookie tins and frozen pies into the waiting arms of her uncle and the Freeman children. Gracie smiled at the way the Freeman girls looked. Marge had done a wonderful job with their hair and had even taken a hand at Bridget's make-up, with simple but stunning results. Not to be outdone by his sisters, Gracie and Trent had gone shopping. In his new black pants and sports jacket, the young man looked positively dashing.

Grabbing a stack of frozen pies from her truck, Gracie was greeted in the kitchen by Pastor Paul. By this time, Don Delano and Lester Twomley had arrived, also bearing pies. Uncle Miltie was carrying a small box but refused to reveal its contents.

Soon all the choir members had arrived. While Marge dressed Trixie in her purple robe and headgear, Gracie and Barb set out plates of sandwiches covered with damp cloths, and baskets of cookies along one countertop.

Marge asked Bridget and Trent to take their sister into the sanctuary while she and the others slipped into their robes. Then, in single file, the choir marched into the sanctuary and took their places behind the crèche.

The sanctuary echoed with whispers and the rustling of coats. The pews were packed as Jeffrey Larson and two other boys, their young faces tight with concentration, ushered people to their seats. Half a dozen individuals shifted at the back, peering over the seated audience, waiting their turn. She saw her uncle swivel and wave Florence Jackson over to occupy a seat he had obviously saved for her.

Pat Allen and her sister were led to third-row seats, immediately beside Rocky Gravino. Abe Wasserman claimed a place next to Herb Bower and his mother.

A parent strode onto the stage area, shifting the three wise men—two of whom were girls—to the right of the crèche and gently discouraging one of the shepherds from sitting on the ceramic donkey. Patsy Clayton, one of the narrators, looked radiantly happy in her turban.

"The kids are behaving awfully well," Marge whispered.

Gracie nodded. But it was Christmastime, after all.

With her head hidden beneath a bright orange turban, Patsy beamed at the audience from her wheelchair. "And she brought forth her first born and wrapped him in swaddling clothes," Patsy began, her small voice quivering. "And laid him in a manger because there was no room at the inn." She stopped, then smiled with all her might. Her parents and grandparents clapped heartily. Gracie's heart rose.

Barb's arm went up and the choir snapped to attention. Just as they began the first bars of *The First Nöel*, Pastor Paul gently prodded a young boy and girl, both wearing white sheets and papier mâché halos, down the center aisle. The girl, whom Gracie recognized as one of the Griswold children, clutched a doll. Its tiny halo fell off before they reached the Nativity scene, causing the first ripple of laughter throughout the audience.

The enactment went well, except for the moment when the innkeeper forgot his lines and left Mary and Joseph standing in the aisle. Fortunately, a prompter quickly whispered the words and, encouraged from the audience by their respective parents, the young couple settled into the manger.

As the choir finished the last verse of *Away in a Manger*, the audience was on its feet, clapping and cheering. The children broke away, some playing hide and seek, others showing off to their parents. Trixie Freeman hugged Marge, then flew into Florence Jackson's arms. Clutching the girl, Flo turned, searching. Finding Gracie, she smiled, eyes filled with gratitude and hope. She rushed over. "I'll never be able to thank you enough," she whispered, her face pressed against Trixie's hair.

Gracie smiled and stroked Trixie's cheek.

Flo gently put the little girl down and embraced Gracie. "Without you, I wouldn't have this second chance . . . these wonderful children in my life." She paused, stepping back, swallowing hard. "You . . . you'll never know how grateful I am."

Heart lurching, Gracie glanced across the milling crowd and spied Trent. He was proudly showing Flo's brooch to Jeffrey Larson and a couple of other boys. Nearby, Bridget chatted happily with a gaggle of young women.

For the first time, both Trent and Bridget's young faces seemed free of worry, a beautiful sight. "There's no need for your gratitude, Flo. I . . . well, the whole town really, owed something to you. You're going to give the Freemans a new and better life. I'm not sure what we'd have done without you."

She smiled at Trixie, who was now spinning around, showing off her costume. "I don't like to think about what might have happened to the children."

Flo's hands rose to her mouth, as though she remembered something. "Uncle Miltie tells me there's even more to thank you for. That it was you who suggested the article to Rocky Gravino." Again she paused, blinking hard. "That was so kind."

"I never wanted to take any credit for that. It was on behalf of all the creative spirits in Mason County that I suggested it."

Florence Jackson gently shook her head. "Oh, Gracie, it's just that . . . you were right all along. I was blind—so consumed by anger—that I couldn't see, but . . ." She glanced around the excited crowd, filling the church with laughter and smiles. "God is watching over me. It's as though my eyes have reopened. I see His loving spirit everywhere now, in you, your uncle, and all your kind friends."

"Come on, Auntie Flo," Trixie said, tugging Florence's hand. "Come and see the baby Jesus, come on, please."

Flo looked at Gracie.

Gracie grinned and waved the two away. Scanning the rest of the noisy crowd, she noticed Emily Wicks. The social worker's eyes met hers. Emily smiled, then continued to speak to her sister.

Laughing and singing *Jingle Bells*, everyone trooped down to the kitchen. Within minutes, the children had attacked the food and most of the adults chatted quietly in small clusters, warming their hands over a cup of mulled cider or egg nog.

"Delicious fudge," Emily Wicks said, a half-bitten piece in her hand. "The cherries are a sinful touch. Or should I say divinely inspired?"

"Thank you," Gracie replied, wanting desperately to ask Emily for her reaction.

"I've had a chance to chat with Mrs. Jackson. You're right. She's a wonderful person. The kids are too busy right now, but I'll make arrangements to speak with them." She slowly chewed on the fudge.

"There's still a lot to do—interviews, paperwork, a few calls—but I think your idea might work. I'll speak to my supervisor tomorrow and we'll take it from there."

Gracie wanted to jump for joy. A line-up had formed in front of the freezer as the choir members handed out pies and received the donations.

"In the meantime, since I know both you and Marge, the kids can stay where they are."

"Oh, thank you, Emily!" she said. Unable to restrain herself, she squeezed the woman in a brief hug. "Bless you!"

"Oh, no. Don't thank me, Gracie," Emily said, slightly embarrassed. "You're the one who deserves all the credit."

35

HALF AN HOUR HAD PASSED since their return from the pageant. Gathered around Gracie's kitchen table, the Freeman children were munching leftover fudge and Christmas tree cookies.

Trixie couldn't stop talking, prattling on about the baby Jesus and how much he enjoyed her gift of frankenstein. Marge and Uncle Miltie both leaned back, sipping coffee while Gracie enjoyed a cup of orange pekoe. Even Gooseberry caught their excitement. He dashed back and forth, batting a small, tinkling ball.

"It's frankin*cense*," Trent corrected Trixie.

"Is everything all right, Trent?" Gracie inquired. "You . . . you seem a bit angry."

The boy scowled, picking at cookie crumbs.

Uncle Miltie turned and touched him on the arm. "What's wrong, son? You look like the big one got away."

"Nothing," Trent said, sounding as if he didn't believe it himself.

Uncle Miltie's eyes narrowed, and he exchanged a puzzled glance with his niece. Gracie shook her head gently, still hoping the boy would tell them what was bothering him. She wasn't sure this was the time to push.

"Well, Miss Trixie," Marge said loudly. "I *love* your dear little angel." She gently tweaked the little girl's nose. "You're awfully lucky, having an Uncle Miltie original."

"That reminds me," Uncle Miltie said, pulling himself up. "Be right back."

Gooseberry watched him leave, then leapt onto his chair.

The group waited as he slowly disappeared into the living room, returning in a couple of minutes. He handed Marge a small package then, giving the cat a gentle nudge, regained his seat. Gooseberry arched his back and stalked over to his dish.

"What's this?" Marge asked.

"It's an early Christmas present. My last piece of pottery."

"What?" Marge and Gracie simultaneously cried.

The old man nodded and flexed his fingers. "The process is really a bit too delicate for me."

"But, Uncle Miltie," Gracie protested. "You seemed to enjoy it so much."

"Learning about it was fun but the actual doing . . ." He shrugged. "What I really enjoyed was working with Flo. So,

I'm going to give her a hand now and then." He glanced at Marge. "Well, aren't you going to open it?"

Trixie jumped down and raced up onto Marge's lap. "Can I help?"

Together, they pulled off a layer of brown paper, then another of bubble wrap. Marge's eyes shone with tears as she gently gripped her gift. It was a ceramic platter, adorned with a stylized willow tree. "The Spirit of Spring," she whispered, clutching the plate to her breast. "Oh, Uncle Miltie, it's beautiful! Isn't it, Trix?"

The little girl grinned, her fingers tracing the decoration of reddish bark and oblong leaves. Marge reached over and embraced Uncle Miltie. "Thank you."

Bridget frowned and peered over her sister's fingers. "That's a willow tree?"

Marge nodded. "Not like ours. It's from the Holy Land."

Gracie decided that the time was right. "I've got a little early Christmas present for you kids, too."

Trixie immediately abandoned Marge's lap for Gracie's. Both Trent and Bridget eyed her.

Gracie squeezed Trixie, inhaling the child's sweet scent. "I think I've found a way for you to keep living at home, together."

"How?" Bridget asked.

"They're not going to break us up?" queried her brother.

Gracie took a deep breath and glanced at Uncle Miltie and Marge. They both smiled. "How would you like it if Mrs. Jackson came to live with you?"

Trent blinked.

"Mrs. Jackson?" Bridget whispered. "You ... you mean it?"

Gracie nodded. "There's still a lot to work out, but the idea is that she'd live with and take care of you. As long as you're all willing."

"She'd live with us?" Trent asked, his face blank with shock. "And we could be together?"

"So long as there were no problems, yes."

"No problems ... oh, no ..." Bridget's voice trailed away. Tears slipped down her cheeks.

"Bridget! Honey, what's wrong?" Gracie asked, leaning forward.

The young woman balled her fists into her eyes. "Oh ... if only we could find the ... ohhh!" She sobbed uncontrollably.

Trent glared at Uncle Miltie. "Well, aren't you going to tell?" he asked.

Uncle Miltie blinked uncomprehendingly. "Tell? Tell what?"

Trent shook his head. "You *know* what I'm talking about."

"Trent, what's going on?" Gracie asked. "I don't think my uncle understands."

"Yes, he does," the boy snapped, slamming the tabletop.

Gooseberry hissed, then streaked from the room. "I saw him with my own eyes."

Mouth open, the old man stared blankly at Trent.

"Saw what?" Marge asked.

"Well?" He jabbed a finger toward Uncle Miltie. "What are you waiting for? Oh . . . never mind. I'll do it myself."

"Trent!" Gracie snapped. "What are you—"

Bang! He was gone.

WHAT WAS *THAT* ALL ABOUT?" Marge demanded, trying to soothe Trixie.

Bridget continued to cry softly.

"What's going on, Bridget?" Gracie asked. "Come on, dear. You can tell us."

The girl raised her swollen eyes but refused to speak.

"Well, I never . . . *never*!" Uncle Miltie sputtered. "What's gotten into that boy?"

Both Gracie and Marge shook their heads.

Bridget opened her mouth.

Slap! He was back again.

"Hold it!" Gracie commanded, rising. She approached the boy and held out her hands. "I'll take that."

Trent paused, a small bundle clutched tightly in his hands. He bit his lip but handed over the package. "Okay, but don't let *him* touch it!" he ordered, jerking a thumb in the direction of Uncle Miltie.

Everyone spoke simultaneously.

"Hey!" Uncle Miltie managed to squeak. His blue eyes opened wide with astonishment.

"Trent!" Gracie cried.

Trent snatched the bundle back from Gracie. In a flash, he'd ripped off the wrapping. With another quick movement, he thrust something colorful into the air. "See?" he crowed, holding high a beautifully painted ceramic angel.

Marge gasped.

"But I thought they were all . . ." Gracie started.

Trixie clapped her hands in excitement.

"Hey!" Uncle Miltie snapped, struggling to his feet. "They're mine! You've got no right . . ."

Trent pulled away the rest of the wrapping to reveal two more identically painted angels. "You said you didn't have any more," Trent said, his tone accusatory. "You lied."

"Now, just wait a minute—" Gracie began.

Uncle Miltie was shaking, his anger clearly visible. "Those are my property, Trent Freeman," he rumbled, cutting off his niece. "You've no right to touch them." He inhaled slowly, regaining control.

Trent stood up to the elderly man's wrath. "You . . . you hid them!" he accused, freckles blazing on his skin. "Because of that old lady's bracelet."

"Bracelet!" Gracie cried.

Uncle Miltie blinked. "Whaaat?"

"You . . . you were going to let Bridget take the blame," Trent continued. "You said there weren't any more angels. I kept waiting for you to bring them out but . . ."

Uncle Miltie slumped into his chair. "Young man, I don't know what you're talking about but I hope you're happy. You've ruined my surprise. These angels are Christmas gifts. One for Gracie, one for Flo and the last one for my little great-nephew, Elmo."

"Christmas gifts," Trent whispered, incredulously. "You . . . you didn't know about—"

Marge finally found her voice. "Wait a second. Wait just one second."

Everyone stared at her. Trixie slipped across the floor and climbed onto Uncle Miltie's lap.

"Well, what on earth do the angels have to do with Mrs. Simmons's bracelet?"

Trent and Bridget exchanged a guilty look.

Bridget sighed heavily. "It's all my fault," she whispered. Trent started to speak. "No, Trent! It's about time." She sniffled and hung her head. "I found it in the hallway, Mrs. Lawrence. I was just coming down the hall to return it when

Mrs. Simmons screamed that it had been stolen. I . . . I guess I panicked. Ran into the kiln room. There was a bunch of statues on the table. I touched one. It was soft, so I stuffed the bracelet into the bottom."

"You did what?" Uncle Miltie blurted.

Bridget nodded, wiped away a tear. "I was going to come back later and get it. I wanted to put it in Mrs. Simmons's room so it could be found."

"But, Bridget, dear," Gracie asked softly, offering the young woman a tissue. "Why didn't you just tell the truth?"

The teen's eyes flashed. "Oh, I wish I had but . . . you see, Mrs. Parks, I was already in trouble. Mrs. Cook caught me . . . smoking in the kiln room. She warned me that the next time I got into trouble, I'd be fired." The young woman appealed to Gracie. "Don't you understand? I didn't think anyone would believe me. I couldn't lose that job, Mrs. Parks! I knew that if anyone ever found out about Aunt Harriet, they'd try and split us up!" She sobbed, then managed to whisper, "I figured if I was working, that would prove that I was capable, responsible enough to take care of my brother and sister."

Bridget succumbed to her tears.

"So, you're the one who smashed my angels at the center," Uncle Miltie said, rocking Trixie slowly back and forth.

The young woman nodded, her sobs increasing. After a moment, she caught her breath. "But I . . . I couldn't find the bracelet! Oh, it was awful! I didn't know what to do."

Gracie reached across and held her hand. "You poor thing," she murmured. "I guess you were pretty frightened."

Uncle Miltie sighed heavily. "Must have been tough," he finally said. "So, you broke into the church and smashed the others."

Bridget shook her head. "Didn't even know they were there until . . ."

"I did it," Trent said. "Bridgie had finally told me what was going on. We couldn't figure out where the statue with the bracelet was. When I saw the angels at the church, during that pie-making thing, I thought I'd found it. Snuck back in later and . . . well, you know." He shook his head. "But I didn't find the bracelet."

"Then we were really stuck," his older sister added.

Trent shifted in his seat. "Yeah. Didn't know what to do until I overheard Chief Bower talking to Uncle Miltie about his angels." His face brightened and he looked at the old man. "Then, I realized that you'd *made* them, not just brought them. And *then* I remembered seeing you hiding something with a halo and wings in your garage, first night I came to shovel. I just figured you knew about the bracelet. Why else keep them secret?" He sighed. "I didn't know they were presents."

His gaze swiveled across to Gracie and he blushed faintly. "I was trying to find them the other night when you came. I . . . wanted to tell you but . . ."

Uncle Miltie grunted. "I figured the garage was the only place Gracie wouldn't look."

Trent bit his lower lip. "Uncle Miltie, I'm . . . I'm really sorry. I shouldn't have called you a liar. I . . . I was just so worried." The boy hung his head. "You've been so nice to me and . . . well . . . I'm really sorry," he whispered.

Everyone was silent. Then, Uncle Miltie carefully put Trixie down and stood. "It's about time we got to the bottom of this, don't you think?"

He slowly made his way into the hallway.

"What's he up to?" Marge whispered.

Gracie shrugged, gaze fixed on the entrance to the kitchen.

Trixie skipped off, shouting, "Wait for me!"

A minute later, they returned. Very deliberately, Uncle Miltie removed a hammer and paper bag from his walker. He put one angel into the bag and offered it, along with the hammer, to Trent.

Trent stared, shook his head and handed them both to his older sister.

Bridget shifted the hammer awkwardly. "Are you sure, Uncle Miltie?"

"Yup."

Bridget glanced at the two women. Both nodded. Marge crossed her fingers.

"Okay," Bridget said, raising her arm.

Wham! The hammer slammed into the paper.

Trent practically ripped the bag from his sister's hands and poured its contents on the table. Everyone dove in, fingers raking the glazed clay bits.

"Oh no! It's not here!" Bridget exclaimed.

"Oh dear," Gracie whispered, glancing at her uncle.

Uncle Miltie sighed, then gently dropped the other angel into the bag.

Wham!

Bridget spilled the contents, so that colored bits raced across the table top. Appearing from nowhere, Gooseberry pounced onto the table, front paws flashing.

Trixie's small fingers jabbed excitedly, shoving broken pieces off the table. "Look, Bridgie! Isn't it pretty?" she said, clutching a gold bracelet, its centerpiece a single, glittering emerald.

"Hurray!" Marge shouted. "Hurray!"

Bridget squealed and hugged her sister. The cat high-tailed it to the top of the refrigerator.

"Yippee!" cried Trent, grabbing the bracelet and handing it to Gracie. "We found it!"

He vigorously shook Uncle Miltie's hand then glanced at his sister.

Bridget took a tentative step. "Mrs. Parks, I . . . don't know what to say." She stroked her younger sister's hair. "Without you, we'd be in big trouble. You . . . you've done so much for us, both of you."

Gracie's heart lurched as she tried to stem her tears. Marge reached across and held her hand while Uncle Miltie cleared his throat.

Trent nodded then jumped in. "You're the best! And we . . . I . . . well, we weren't honest with you." He lowered his eyes. "That was wrong, Mrs. Parks, Uncle Miltie. I know. I wanted to talk, to tell you, but we were so afraid . . ."

Gracie wiped a tear and held out her arms. Trixie flew into them before Gracie blinked. The older children smiled and shyly shuffled over. Tears streaming down her cheeks, Gracie embraced them all.

"It's going to be all right, Mrs. Parks," Trent whispered. "Isn't it?"

"Hey? What about us?" Marge and Uncle Miltie asked, arms spread.

The kids rushed into their embrace.

"I think so, Trent." Gracie smiled. "Our prayers have been answered, thanks be to God. I'm sure everything *is* going to be all right."

"I don't know how we'll ever be able to thank you," Bridget said, gently kissing each woman on the cheek. Then, she threw her arms around Uncle Miltie's neck while Trixie clutched at his knees. "I'll come and clean your house, every week. Yours, too, Mrs. Lawrence."

"And I . . . I'll shovel both your walks and driveways for free," Trent added. "In the summer, I'll do your lawns."

"Thank you, my dears, but that won't be necessary," Gracie said, her heart bursting at the sight of the three happy children. Teary, Marge just shook her head. The Freemans watched Gracie. "Simply remember this: What you are is God's gift to you."

Uncle Miltie nodded, then finished the saying, "What you become is your gift to God."

"Amen," Marge said. Then she clapped her hands. "This calls for a celebration!"

"Ice cream sundaes, everyone?"

The kids applauded.

"Good," Gracie said. "You get started while I let Herb know about the bracelet."

As she reached for the phone, her uncle spoke. "Well, I'll be," he said, touching the remaining angel.

The others looked at him.

"There's a guardian angel left for Elmo."

"Don't really think he needs it," Trent said, ice cream tub in his hands.

There was an odd silence. Gooseberry chose that moment to jump off the fridge and brush up against the boy's leg.

The young man blushed. "Well, if you ask me, he's already got three."

Gracie's Piquant Pork Chops

- ✓ 4 pork chops (approximately 1 inch thick)
- ✓ 1 clove garlic, peeled and finely chopped
- ✓ 3 tablespoons chili sauce
- ✓ 3 tablespoons cider vinegar
- ✓ 2 teaspoons Worcestershire sauce
- ✓ 1/4 teaspoon dry mustard
- ✓ 1/4 teaspoon salt
- ✓ small chicken bouillon cube

Combine the garlic, chili sauce, cider vinegar, Worcestershire sauce and dry seasonings into a dish. Place the pork chops in this mixture and turn them over once or twice. Then leave them to marinate in the refrigerator, covered lightly, for an hour.

When the time is up, remove the pork chops—saving the marinade—and brown in a hot, lightly greased pan. Remove pan from the heat when the pork chops are done.

Next, in a small saucepan, boil 1/2 cup of water with the bouillon cube. Add it to the reserved marinade, stir and pour over pork chops. Now cover the pan tightly and bake in a 350-degree oven for about an hour, or until tender.

Gracie says, "Just a few minutes before it's ready to serve, I like to spoon three or four dollops of a good quality bottled salsa into the sauce and stir it around. I use the mild variety—not only because Uncle Miltie prefers it, but because it makes for a better contrast to the seasonings already in the dish.

"Buttered limas are a nice accompaniment, and a quick corn bread complements both of them."

About the Author

NICOLA FURLONG makes every effort to steal time away from cycling, playing ice hockey, growing perennials from seed and devouring chocolates (mostly devouring chocolates) to slip a snippet of mystery and suspense writing into each day.

Born in Edmonton, Alberta, the sixth of eight children, Nicola was raised in the Canadian provinces of Saskatchewan, Ontario and Prince Edward Island. She received a degree in fine arts and psychology from Carleton University in Ottawa, and then, following several older siblings, scrambled up the bureaucratic ladder with the Canadian government. After the publication of a number of essays, articles and short stories, her first mystery novel, *Teed Off!*, was published in 1996. Later that year, she left the civil service behind to concentrate on writing fiction and also serving as a consultant to fisheries and environmental organizations. Her second novel, *A Hemorrhaging of Souls*, was published in 1998. She recently finished a suspense thriller entitled *Thy Will Be Done* and is currently researching a sequel.

Nicola lives in Sidney-by-the-Sea, a small town on southern Vancouver Island, British Columbia. You can visit Nicola's Web site at www.nicolafurlong.com.

A NOTE FROM THE EDITORS

This original Guideposts Book was created by the Book and Inspirational Media Division of the company that publishes *Guideposts,* a monthly magazine filled with true stories of hope and inspiration.

Guideposts is available by subscription. All you have to do is write to Guideposts, 39 Seminary Hill Road, Carmel, New York 10512. When you subscribe, each month you can count on receiving exciting new evidence of God's presence, His guidance and His limitless love for all of us.

Guideposts Books are available on the World Wide Web at www.guidepostsbooks.com. Follow our popular book of devotionals, *Daily Guideposts,* and read excerpts from some of our best-selling books. You can also send prayer requests to our Monday morning Prayer Fellowship and read stories from recent issues of our magazines, *Guideposts, Angels on Earth,* and *Guideposts for Teens.*